EXTRACURRICULAR

BOOK 3 OF 3 EPISODIC NOVELS

JOSIE BROWN

A BOOK BY

SIGNAL PRESS

"Master storyteller of the competitively elite, Totlandia's Josie Brown graduates from strollers and playgroups to the high stakes game of college admissions in this captivating tale of trickery, deceit, and unrequited love. Told across three episodic novels, meet the movers, the shakers, and the dirty-deal makers that, together, establish a page-turning premise to carry us forward: It's the tiny twists of fate that change us. A++ for *Extracurricular.*"

—Julie Valerie, author of *Holly Banks Full of Angst* and the *Village of Primm* series

"Josie Brown brings it, in this ripped-from-the-headlines romp of a novel set in the world of academia and its shadow world – extracurricular activities that may not be legal. It has romance and intrigue, and a pace that doesn't let up. Highly entertaining. Sure to delight Brown's legions of fans."

—Eileen Goudge, New York Times bestselling author
of *Garden of Lies* and *The Diary*

"Delicious, hilarious, and addictive, *Extracurricular* has all the hallmarks of a classic Josie Brown book: fleshed-out, juicy characters, a to-die-for plot, and a ripped-from-the-headlines premise. I absolutely loved it and must read the entire series!"

—Samantha M. Bailey, author, *Woman on the Edge*

"Sharp, smart, and sexy, Brown's timely new series about the cut-throat world of college admissions is a must-read. As always, Brown's cast of characters is a delicious mix of sweethearts, scoundrels and the just plain morally corrupt. Never predictable, *Extracurricular* is immensely enjoyable."

—Meredith Schorr, author of *The Boyfriend Swap* and the *Blogger Girl* series

"Dirty little secrets have a way of catching up with us. *Housewife Assassin* and *Totlandia* fans rejoice! Josie Brown has a new trail of secrets, lies, and parents behaving badly—and you're gonna love it. Ripped from the headlines, *Extracurricular* delivers the perfect summer read on just how far some people will go, no matter the cost, to get exactly what they want."

—Jen Tucker, author, *The Day I Wore My Panties Inside Out*, and Chick Lit Central columnist

"Josie Brown has hit it out of the ballpark with this timely tale of family, friends, love and the morally corrupt. As always, Ms. Brown's writing is sharp, smart, and oh-so witty. She'll have you laughing out loud one minute and cringing the next at her characters' antics and comments. Filled with twist and turns and complicated emotions that lead to decisions that play pivotal moments in the characters lives, this story will reach out and grab your attention from page one and not let go until the end. I now sit on tenterhooks awaiting the next release to find out who will be going down and who will be saved."

—Gail Chianese, author, *Love Runs Deep*

CHAPTER 1

The official time of Lavinia Thorpe's death was Thursday at 7:55 in the evening.

The hospital's paperwork took an hour. During the process, Lavinia's doctor had assured Audrey Thorpe that her mother's body would be taken to the hospital's morgue until the family's designated funeral home retrieved it.

Audrey, her husband Daniel, and the McKittridge children—seventeen-year-old twins Charly and Chuck, and twelve-year-old Noah—were home by ten. Stunned by grief, their daughter Charly and her brothers went up to their rooms.

Audrey dreaded the next task: breaking the news to Lavinia's closest friends—Maggie and her daughter, Tallulah Wishart; Maude and Reggie Thackeray and their daughter, Bliss; and Harris Blanchard and his wife, Tracy. Bliss and Tallulah were Audrey's dearest friends, as was Davis Wong, who viewed Lavinia as his surrogate mother since she'd found him living on the streets.

By providing him a full scholarship to Ashbury Academy—the private school she'd founded and served as its headmistress—his life had been forever altered. He was now one of the world's most sought-after film directors.

But Audrey's very first call went to Gemma Sisley. Her father, Grayson Sisley, would have wanted to know about Lavinia's passing, but Audrey knew Gemma would best know when to break the news to him, considering that both would still be in shock over their own tragedy: Gemma's husband, Darius Calder, had been murdered less than twenty-four hours earlier.

Like Audrey, Gemma was consumed by her grief. Together, the dear friends sobbed over their losses.

After these initial calls, it dawned on Audrey that the staff at Ashbury Academy should also be informed as soon as possible. Lavinia had been the institution's heart and soul.

"Let's split up the list," Daniel suggested.

"I'd appreciate that." Audrey's words were weighted with her pain. "Let's ask them to call the parents of students in their first class with the news."

"Will do." Daniel hesitated, then added, "We should also inform the trustee board."

"I'll let you do that. In fact, you should start with them, I guess. I'll leave it to your discretion whether or not to mention Darius as well."

"I think I should," Daniel replied. "It's my fiduciary responsibility since he sat on the school's board."

Audrey stifled a wince. It's why she'd kept her promise to Lavinia and never mentioned her mother's illness to Daniel. Had he disclosed it to the board, Lavinia would not have had the bittersweet pleasure of avoiding the inevitable pity and tears of AA's staff and students during those final months of her life.

I know because my grieving dismayed her.

Audrey stared down at the staff directory, but her eyes couldn't focus through the haze of her tears. Finally, she sighed. "I'll take everyone whose last name begins with A through L. You can take M through Z." She made a screenshot of the directory with her phone and texted it to him.

Miranda D'Arcy was the third name on Audrey's call sheet. She skipped it, though, knowing that AA's college admissions counselor would also be on Daniel's list of board members.

However, when she realized Egan Gable's name was on her call sheet, she decided he should hear the news from her, not Daniel.

After all, he was the twins' biological father.

And the last person he'd want to hear about Lavinia's death from was the man who was raising them as his own.

***

"Faster.... HARDER.... *DEEPER!* Come on, big boy— break me in half! *YES! YES!*" Miranda D'Arcy barked out her commands like a Visigoth general during the sacking of Rome.

When it came to sex, Egan didn't like taking directions —let alone from a woman he despised.

He'd been dismayed when, almost two hours after he'd left her, she actually followed through on delivering the check she promised—from a non-profit company called The Best Face Forward Club. Until then, he'd anxiously been staring out the window, hoping that, by some miracle, she'd have second thoughts about it.

Heaven knows he'd had them.

Buena Vista Park was directly across the street from Egan's apartment. Her car had pulled up into one of the parking spots abutting the greenbelt. As she got out of the car and crossed the street, he'd noticed another auto pulling up as well: a Camry, but a much more recent model than his parents' car. It pulled into an empty space two away from hers.

The driver turned off the engine but sat in the car. Only the streetlight illuminated the figure inside.

Whereas Egan had once considered Miranda a possible love interest, the revelation of her connivery toward Lavinia and Ashbury Academy had killed any inkling of attraction he'd briefly felt toward her, let alone friendship. He had only acquiesced to the tryst as a way to assure her that he would play along with the scheme she'd roped him into while threatening to tell Daniel about Egan and Audrey's one-night stand, now so many years ago.

If Daniel found out, he'd confront Audrey about it.

Immediately, she'd realize that Egan had blabbed their secret to Miranda. She'd panic that Daniel would recognize the truth about the twins. And Audrey would hate Egan even more than she did now—if that were possible.

Caught between two undesirable outcomes, Egan had made up his mind that this tryst with Miranda would be a swift and unmemorable slam-bam-thank-you-ma'am. That way, she'd never suggest a second go-round. Better to have her think of him as a lousy lover.

To his dismay, Miranda had other ideas about the evening. Immediately, she took the lead: yanking off his jeans, shoving him down against the couch, and mounting him without even bothering to strip off anything other than the thong she wore under her designer dress.

Egan had never been into rough sex. He was a romantic at heart. Besides, he liked to please women, both in and out of the bedroom. To him, flirtation was an art form. He strove to create a multi-sensory experience with words, gazes, smiles, and a well-placed hand—say, the mere stroke on a woman's arm. Should the woman respond positively (and odds were she would), he took consummate care in each step of their lovemaking. The foreplay was gentle and thorough. Any words spoken were husky with yearning or filled with desire. When their eyes met, his gaze vowed the depth of his desire.

He never forced, he coaxed. His climaxes weren't quick, and his lover was assured of many.

He left his conquests satiated of their shared lust.

Or so he believed anyway.

But Miranda was another story. Throughout the love bout, her naughty talk was taunts tainted with filth and innuendo, each one more despicable than the last. It sickened him to the point that he felt like throwing up, but he resisted the urge, should she find it a turn-on.

And despite his vow to hold back on any orgasm, as she tightened around his shaft, inevitably, nature took its course.

Thankfully, his orgasm came simultaneously with hers. Had it not, Egan had no doubt she'd be cruel enough to leave him blue-balled.

With a gasp, Miranda collapsed, "Well, now you are certainly earning your keep!" She raised her face to his. Batting her eyes, she added, "You're ready to go again, right?"

Aw, hell...NO. "Look, it's...been a long day. Maybe you should take off—"

He stifled a groan as she cupped him.

"Oh, look!" Miranda giggled, delighted. "You're not tired at all. You're rarin' to go!"

As she leaped off the couch, she grabbed her purse. "First, I've got to make a pit stop. You know, freshen up." She sauntered off toward the bathroom.

And not a second too soon. Egan's phone buzzed. The caller ID showed one letter:

A

Audrey.

It was silly, he knew, to identify her on his phone that way. But considering their secret—especially after what he'd heard tonight—he was too ashamed to claim their relationship, even in the privacy of his phone.

Why is she calling—now, of all times?

As quickly as he could, he tapped open the phone and whispered, "Hi."

"I wanted you to be the first to know. Lavinia died tonight." Audrey's voice reeked of bleakness.

Her words hit him so hard that he had to stifle a groan. "How…"

"Heart attack." Audrey's sigh was part sob too. "But I'm sure that all the stress over the trustee board gamesmanship and her cancer and its treatment played a hand in it."

Egan flinched at the thought of the role the board had played in Lavinia's demise.

She's right. And things will only get worse if Miranda gets her way.

I have to tell Audrey about Miranda's scheme.

Urgently, he whispered, "Audrey, listen—"

"Egan, sorry, but I really can't talk now. I have to call

others on the staff. Daniel is helping me in this endeavor—and he's calling board members too." Egan could hear her choking back her tears. "I…I just wanted you to hear it first, and from me."

She hung up before he could say anything to stop her.

There was a time Miranda would have never assumed that Egan Gable would see her *naked*. Then again, who'd have thought that egotist would live up to his own hype?

It took Miranda all of five minutes to wash up. The next five were spent admiring her tits and ass in the bathroom mirror. If her mother had taught her one thing, it was that men abhorred naughty bits that sagged. Both body parts had undergone extensive plastic surgery, but it was worth it. Diet and exercise only went so far.

Thank goodness, she'd done so before pitching Lavinia on hiring her as Ashbury Academy's college counseling consultant.

Even before her divorce—in fact, it's why her husband left her—for Miranda, sex was usually a random pickup: quick, down and dirty, no commitments. These past two months, her tepid trysts with Jess Smallwood had only been a means to an end. It got her on AA's trustee board. From there, she could contain—and better yet, *control*—any issues that might arise from her illegal acts involving her college admissions concierge program.

And now that the FBI was involved, undoubtedly the shit would soon be hitting the fan.

When it did, she planned on being far away.

Too bad she couldn't take the best lay of her life with her—

Egan.

Sadly, she'd have to leave him behind so that he could take the fall for her.

The thought of visiting him in prison for conjugal sex made her all hot and bothered again.

That fantasy was still rolling around in her head when she realized her cell phone was buzzing. The caller ID read:

D McKittridge

Interesting. What could he possibly want this late at night?

"Daniel? How may I help you?"

"Hello, Miranda. Thanks for picking up so late." To her ears, he sounded defeated.

It would be too delicious to hear that he was covertly calling her about helping him get his deadbeat boy, Chuck, into her concierge program.

In anticipation that this was the case, she cooed, "No problem."

"I'm calling all board members as well as the staff with the sad news that Lavinia passed away tonight."

Emotions roiled through Miranda. Shock was replaced by guilt.

Not for long, though. Relief quickly took its place.

Lavinia's trust had been misplaced, but it had worked in Miranda's favor.

Finally, Miranda was filled with elation. With Lavinia's demise, she could be bolder in courting parents gullible enough to buy into her illegal college admissions scheme.

Granted, she'd still have to be cautious about it so as not to alert those who could call it into question publicly—

Like Daniel.

"I'm stunned," Miranda murmured. "Truly, Daniel… Your news—well, it cuts me to the quick."

"I'll pass along your regrets to Audrey," he replied.

He sounds as if he means it, the fool. "Yes, please do. And tell her that if there's anything I can do…" For effect, Miranda let her voice trail off.

"Thank you. Have a good night."

Hell yeah, I will.

Jubilantly, she tossed her phone in her purse. She was about to walk out of the room when her phone buzzed again.

As she suspected, it was a text from Seamus McCoppin. As Lavinia's prime nemesis on the trustee board, he'd be raring to go on a scheme to take control—not only of the board but the school as well. He wrote:

**Lavinia RIP. Must meet to discuss the school's need to transition. Zingari: 1pm tomorrow.
BTW I have a client referral for you.**

Miranda wrote back:

See you there.

Forty-eight hours ago, Miranda planted the seed that Seamus should oust Lavinia and put her in the headmistress' place—at least, temporarily.

Doing so would have made for the ideal set-up: Miranda could recruit new clients and control the trustee board. No need to have a replay of the Bobbit-Hennings fiasco.

But since then, Miranda's life had changed drastically —and for the worst.

The FBI was now her constant companion.

Miranda needed that coverage now more than ever: to cover her tracks, what with the Feds onto her, and thinking they'd turned her.

Lavinia's sudden death relieved Seamus of the need for a vicious power play.

But no way was she going to let him position her as Ashbury Academy's permanent Head of School. When they meet at lunch, she'd inform him that her private consulting business was too lucrative to give up; that she wouldn't mind stepping in as Lavinia's temporary replacement so that a search committee could take its time to find just the right fit for his vision of AA.

That way, I can manage the board while I plan my exit from everything: the business, the country even.

I'll just disappear with all my money.

Maybe Egan would like to go with me.

It would beat the alternative: a perp walk in front of the whole school.

Not that he knew that. Nor would she tell him—not yet, anyway.

Egan was used to leaving women with smiles on their faces, so he wasn't surprised when Miranda returned with a smug grin on her face.

What did perturb him was the casual way in which she

snapped her fingers at him. "Time for a change of venue, big boy."

Before he had a chance to respond, she yanked him to his feet, dragging him with her toward his bedroom.

The thought of having sex again with the bitch who was bound and determined to dismantle Lavinia's legacy —and doing so in his bed, no less—so revolted Egan that he actually thought he'd never sleep a wink in there again.

I just moved into this apartment, he thought miserably. I'll have to move again. Worse, she'll do the same thing in the next apartment...

I'm trapped! Miranda is my inferno...

Like hell, I am.

Egan stopped short, taking her by surprise. Before she could object, he growled, "Okay, sure. But this time, we do it my way."

She frowned at his tone. But before she could respond, he grabbed her by her shoulders and turned her so that she faced the wall. He forced her forearms against it. Then he kicked her legs apart.

Annoyed, she declared, "What the—"

But then he walloped her ass, and she took the hint she'd better brace herself. "Ready to play *really* rough?" he murmured in her ear.

Miranda's eyes widened. "Frankly, I didn't know you had it in you," she cooed. "Sure! *Bring it on.*"

As he entered her from behind, she squealed delightedly. He was tall enough that she had to stand on her tiptoes.

Let's get this over with...

Each thrust compounded his anger. Once again, he held off as long as he could—

Until nature took its course.

Exhausted, he collapsed onto her.

Miranda, too, was spent.

As soon as he could, he staggered to pick up his clothes.

Miranda frowned. "Wait—where are you going?"

"Away—from you," he retorted as he zipped up his pants.

Hotly, she exclaimed, "But I'm not finished with you!"

Egan snickered. "Let me make myself clear, Miranda: *being with you repulses me.* If you insist on making it part and parcel of our so-called 'deal,' I'll tear up the check, and that will be the end of it. I will also deny any lies you spread about Audrey or me. In fact, I'll stand up on Ashbury Academy's bell tower with a megaphone and announce your scheme to the world. Do you understand me?"

She glowered back, but she kept her mouth shut.

In no time, he tossed on his shirt and jacket and was through the front door, slamming it behind him.

Why you son of a bitch!

Miranda was still shaking as she snatched her clothes off the floor and then walked over to Egan's desk, where he'd tossed the check.

He did it to taunt me, she fumed. He wants me to pick it up and tear it into tiny little pieces.

But doing so would get him off the hook with the Feds.

Back at the restaurant, when she'd made her deal with Egan, she'd delighted at having him at her beck and call—emotionally and physically. On the drive over to Egan's house, she'd crowed at the thought that the FBI might be listening in. Despite Special Agent Lionel Polk's tough talk about seeing right through her, she could see it in his eyes: she intrigued him. While in the throes of lust, it thrilled her to know Lionel had heard every word—and every grunt.

No doubt, he also heard Egan's cruel put-down.

That son of a bitch humiliated me, Miranda fumed.

She had some consolation. To that extent, she'd already put a very large nail in the coffin of his professional life: Just that morning she—that is, Mandy Blackwell—had signed, in triplicate, the settlement papers for her lawsuit against Egan and his publisher, Signal Press. It had brought yet another half a million dollars to her fly-the-coop account.

To keep the FBI off my back as long as possible, I have to keep Egan in play.

Then, when the time is right, I'll take him down.

And at the same time, I'll ruin Audrey's perfect little world.

In case Miranda was looking out the window, Egan walked into the park, only to detour onto another path that circled around, putting him back in front of the apartment building.

From behind one of the park's behemoth live oaks, he watched as, ten minutes later, Miranda left too.

As she drove off, the car that had arrived immediately after her now started its engine.

Egan watched as it followed her path: north on Buena Vista Avenue, making a quick left westward onto Haight, and then a sharp right onto Central Avenue.

Interesting, Egan mused. Apparently, the driver never got out of the car.

If Egan were lucky, maybe the mysterious car's driver shared Egan's fantasy: doing away with Miranda.

One could only hope.

He went back up to his apartment. When he walked by the sofa, he pointedly turned his head to look away, disgusted by the thought of what had transpired less than an hour before.

I'll have Goodwill tow it out of here as soon as possible, he thought.

Egan walked over to his desk. He stared down at Miranda's check:

Two hundred and forty-five thousand dollars.

Thirty-five thousand times seven students.

Depending on the schools Charly and Chuck chose, it would almost cover two four-year college tuitions—

One for each.

This is to be the legacy I leave my children, he thought.

And knowing Miranda, there will be other parents buying into her program until the final SAT deadline.

Jesus—what if Miranda pitches her scheme to some parent who decides to tell a cop?

She'll take me down with her.

What will Chuck and Charly think of me then?

The thought shamed him.

Still, it could not deter him from what he knew he had to do, first thing in the morning: deposit her check into his bank account.

Egan signed the back of it and then slipped it into an envelope.

I have to spend the money. I have no choice.

To this end, he filled out a blank check from his account and put it in the envelope too, which went in the pocket of his favorite jacket.

Exhausted, Egan went to bed, where he spent the night tossing and turning.

Finding himself up at the crack of dawn, Egan went ahead and got dressed. His destination was Ashbury Academy, but first, he stopped off at his bank's ATM machine to deposit the check from the Best Face Forward Club. His heart dropped into the pit of his stomach as the check rolled through his fingers and into the machine.

When Egan reached AA, he found the front door locked. He'd never been the first teacher on campus. But since all teachers had keys to the front door, he let himself in.

He had a hard time passing Lavinia's office without glancing over. Unless she'd been in a private meeting, her habit was to leave the door open. Instinctively, he looked to see her smiling face.

No more, he realized.

He stopped at the receptionist's desk. Clare, who had been at the school since its inception, would soon be in, he knew.

He took a blank sheet of paper from the scrap bin behind her desk and scribbled a quick note. He knew the words he wrote would be small solace for her grief, but perhaps it would help to some extent.

Folding it, he slipped it into the envelope and placed it partially under her keyboard.

He headed for the teachers' lounge. The unwritten rule was for the first one through the door to make the coffee.

He knew where Cornell kept his French press and stash of private label beans. He doubted the chemistry teacher would balk just this once at the notion of sharing it with the rest of the teachers, considering the sadness and gravity of the occasion.

Because it was a Friday teachers' workday, Egan made up his mind he'd nudge the teachers into a discussion of how to handle their grieving students come Monday. Beyond that, he couldn't predict what might happen to staff morale.

Lavinia had been the school's heart, soul, and mind. Now that she would no longer walk through the teachers' lounge, eyes glistening with humor and a broad smile on her face, there was no one there to inspire AA's teachers.

He hoped the trustee board would do a thorough search to find someone who would at least do their best to fill Lavinia's shoes.

And more importantly, make her vision the school's permanent mission.

Somehow, he doubted it.

Still, he'd do his best to make it happen.

He owed Lavinia that much.

CHAPTER 2

FBI Special Agent SallyAnne Jagger arrived at the bureau's San Francisco office just as the sun rose over the horizon.

She too had spent a sleepless night.

She was still in shock over the kiss that she and her investigative partner, Lionel Porter Polk VII, had shared the night before while transcribing their report from the sting that Miranda had set up at the chic Presidio Heights restaurant, Spruce.

What had precipitated the kiss—and Lionel's immediate apology for overstepping such a personal boundary —was what SallyAnne could only deduce as jealousy on his part. A stranger had tried to pick up SallyAnne as they were surveilling Miranda and her clients, Seamus and Gretchen McCoppin.

The man had been persistent.

Granted, he'd also been drunk.

Still, SallyAnne had been flattered—especially when

she realized he was Egan Gable—the author of her favorite book, *Extracurricular.*

On the other hand, Lionel had been rude in his attempt to shoo Egan away.

Unfortunately, Egan had picked up on the fact that they'd been eyeing Miranda and the McCoppins.

Such irony! Egan knew them well because he was now teaching at Ashbury Academy. And as it turned out, he was also the teacher liaison to AA's trustee board—one of the reasons his voice had sounded so familiar to Sally-Anne, since the FBI had been listening in on the meetings.

Before they could stop him, he had tottered over to their table.

The good news: as promised, Miranda set up the McCoppins to implicate themselves.

The bad news: Miranda was successful in recruiting Egan for her illicit activities.

Although he'd initially balked at her offer to act as proctor for the students in her concierge program—in other words, take their tests for them—he'd finally agreed. Apparently, Egan was desperate for money. Not only that, Miranda was holding some threat over his head. Their conversation didn't reveal exactly what.

Because of SallyAnne's nostalgia for Egan's book, she despised Miranda even more for the hold she had over Egan.

As she rounded the corner to her cubicle, she caught sight of Lionel in the break room. He was deep in discussion with the tech agent also assigned to the case, Riley Kemp.

At that moment, Lionel looked over and saw her too. He smiled.

SallyAnne felt a blush creeping up her neck. She forced a smile onto her lips and strode over. "I guess if I'm ever to make it in earlier than you, I'll just have to put a cot in my cubicle."

"I…couldn't sleep," he admitted.

Because of what happened between us last night?

She longed to ask him that.

"Yeah, well, it seems that none of us is going to get much sleep over these next few months," Riley crowed. "This case is heating up by the nanosecond!"

SallyAnne frowned. "I can only imagine, from what you texted Lionel last night."

"Oh, you ain't heard nothin' yet," he assured her. "Besides the X-rated sexfest, they were alerted that AA's headmistress passed last night!"

"What?" Lionel and SallyAnne exclaimed in unison.

Riley nodded toward the conference room. "I've got the whole audio cued up so that you can hear it yourself."

As much as SallyAnne ached for a cup of coffee, she followed Riley down the hall.

She hadn't realized Lionel was still in the break room until she sat down. A moment later he walked in, carrying two mugs of coffee. He placed one in front of her. The coffee was light, just as she liked it. One sip told her he'd somehow picked up on the fact that she doctored her coffee with two cubes of sugar.

"Thank you," she stammered.

He grinned shyly. "My pleasure."

Don't read anything into this, SallyAnne warned herself. It's nothing more than a random act of kindness.

But she knew better.

Her previous partner, also male, had automatically

assumed she'd bring him a cup whenever she got one for herself. Immediately, she cured him of that expectation by substituting salt for sugar.

When she and Lionel had first partnered up, she'd never offered to get his coffee. He'd followed her lead in forgoing beverage requests. Still, she too had watched him order coffee numerous times over the past few years and knew he took his black.

One good turn deserved another, she thought.

But something much bigger than a coffee run. As with his gesture, it had to be something implicit of how she hoped the kiss hadn't ruined their friendship.

In fact, it would express the opposite: that the intimacy they'd shared had strengthened their relationship.

That she thought of him as more than just a friend.

I guess I have Egan to thank for motivating Lionel to show his feelings for me, SallyAnne reasoned.

All the more reason it pained SallyAnne that the FBI sting had embroiled Egan in Miranda's illegal activities.

She didn't know what Miranda had on Egan, but whatever it was, she hoped it wasn't illegal.

If it turned out it wasn't, SallyAnne vowed to do what she could to help Egan get out from under Miranda's thumb.

The agents listened as Miranda ecstatically moaned through her first sex bout with Egan. At one point, Sally-Anne had to smack Riley on the shoulder to stop him from snickering.

They also listened to Miranda's conversation with

Daniel. Although Miranda's words were drenched in sympathy, SallyAnne muttered, "She's putting on a show."

Lionel looked surprised. "How can you tell?"

SallyAnne shrugged. "Because whenever she talks to, or about, Audrey, she has a distinct edge to her voice."

Lionel thought for a moment. "You know, you're right! Why do you think that is?"

"It might have something to do with the fact that Audrey is everything Miranda isn't: kind, thoughtful, and morally sound."

Riley, who'd kept his eyes closed through the cacophony of ecstatic moans, opened one long enough to declare, "I'll bet she's hated Audrey since they were in high school."

SallyAnne and Lionel exchanged glances. That thought had never occurred to either of them.

"That would mean she was also in school with Tallulah Wishart and Bliss Thackeray Belluci," Lionel pointed out. "As of yet, none of these women seem to have warmed up to her, let alone mention the good old days."

"If it's because they can't stand her, I'm sure that drives her up a wall," SallyAnne retorted.

"By the way, Melamed left word that the surveillance subpoenas came through on Jammerhead, Nira Patel, and Jess Smallwood," Lionel announced. "We should have the ones for the McCoppins by tomorrow. Miranda gets the SAT key next Friday. Until then, we're to babysit her as she makes calls to her SoCal clients so that we can record her reiterating the terms."

Riley added, "Tech will start monitoring these witnesses, as well as their college-bound children, for messages and conversations with Miranda."

"Great," Lionel replied. "And after Melamed reads our report about Egan Gable crashing yesterday's meeting between Miranda and the McCoppins, he'll ask for a surveillance subpoena for him as well." Noting Sally-Anne's frown, he added, "I have to give your boy Egan some credit for at least one thing. Despite the fringe benefits, he shut down Miranda quick enough."

"He's not my boy," SallyAnne sniffed. "And he certainly didn't appreciate being sexually abused by that conniving *felon*."

As soon as the remark was out of her mouth, SallyAnne regretted it. The last thing she needed was for Lionel to think she had a soft spot for Egan. He was jealous enough as it was.

On the other hand, maybe that was a good thing.

"Sure, okay, if you say so." He looked at his watch. "I'll call her attorney at eight so that he can inform her to expect us by nine." Lionel grimaced at the thought.

Miranda is just as deplorable to him as she is to me, SallyAnne realized.

It was comforting to know.

After flinging open her front door, Miranda beckoned the FBI agents to enter. "Sorry, just got up. I had *such* a busy night! But you know that already, don't you?"

Seeing SallyAnne's blush, she added, "*Ooooh,* I hope you're not too jealous. I mean, it doesn't bother *me* in the least that Egan tried to pick you up. His douche-bag lounge lizard come-ons are part of his charm, don't you think?" Before SallyAnne could respond, Miranda nodded toward Lionel. "Don't answer that. No need to get Handsome here all uptight over it." Sauntering ahead of them, she cooed, "Haven't even had my coffee yet, but it's percolating. It's the only thing that wakes me up."

To make her point, she turned around and stretched her arms toward the ceiling. Her sweet pink baby doll silk robe rose high enough for a peek of the heart-shaped trimmed nether region of her naked body.

Noting the red creeping into Lionel's face, Miranda giggled. "Oh...*I'm sorry!* I didn't mean to embarrass you." She shrugged. "But it's not as if you haven't seen one before, am I right?" She nodded toward SallyAnne. "Like hers, maybe?"

Fists clenched, SallyAnne took a step forward.

Lionel moved between them. "Why don't you get dressed, Miranda? You've got a long day ahead of you."

"I'll say I have!" She reached for her phone. Pointing to the screen, she exclaimed, "Seamus McCoppin texted me last night. Wants to meet for lunch. Says he has a recruit for me." She shrugged. "But you know that already, don't you, since you have my phone bugged? I guess my car is as well."

Neither agent said anything.

"Hey, no fair," Miranda pouted. "Just by 'fessing up about Seamus I opened my kimono to *you*." To make her point, she untied her robe and flung it open, then giggled as Lionel's jaw dropped open. "Shouldn't you do the same?"

Lionel grabbed her by the shoulders and goose-stepped her down the hall. When he came to what looked like the master bedroom, he tossed her in there, slamming the door shut.

"You've got five minutes to put on something decent," he declared. "If not, your immunity is null and void."

"You can't do that!" Miranda shouted.

SallyAnne detected the panic in her voice. Her guess was that Miranda was straining to hear if they felt she stepped over the line.

She had, and they were tired of her antics. SallyAnne retorted, "Yes we can—*and we will.* We already have you on audio recruiting AA parents for your so-called concierge program. And we also have your list of Southern California concierge clients. Granted, having you call and confirm their participation would have been icing on the cake, but if you're not willing to play ball, so be it. They'll fold like a house of cards, with or without your cooperation. And as far as we're concerned, the more time you spend behind bars, the better."

Silence.

Lionel and SallyAnne's eyes met. Miranda's apartment was on the building's penthouse level. *Surely, she hadn't jumped...*

Lionel tried the doorknob. It was locked.

He had just positioned his shoulder against the door to ram it when it opened. He stumbled through the opening. Luckily, he righted himself before sprawling onto the floor.

Miranda was standing far enough to one side that she avoided a collision.

She'd changed into brown leather pants, a beige cowl-neck sweater, and beige Louboutins. Her makeup was minimal, and her hair was swept into a chignon.

Lowering her eyes, she whispered, "I'm sorry. My behavior was uncalled for."

Neither agent said anything. Finally, Lionel muttered, "Just don't let it happen again."

Meekly, Miranda nodded.

Satisfied, Lionel turned toward the living room.

SallyAnne allowed Miranda to walk past her, which was how she was able to catch Miranda's ever-so-slight triumphant smile.

CHAPTER 3

That her mother's death had occurred during a two-day student recess for a teacher's workday adjacent to a weekend seemed right to Audrey. Perhaps it was existentially planned on Lavinia's part: as if she instinctively knew her family, friends, and school community would need these extra days to process their shock over her loss.

When Audrey woke up, the sun was just peeking up over the East Bay hills. Daniel must have felt her stir because his arm went around her waist, pulling her closer to him.

She nestled in for a moment, but then sighed. "I should get up. I have to take care of Lavinia."

By that, she meant setting a time to meet the director of the funeral home regarding the cremation; getting an urn for the ashes; arranging a time and place for Lavinia's private memorial; and inviting the school community and others who loved Lavinia to the public Celebration of Life service.

Daniel sat up in bed. "Of course. I'll go too."

"But…what about the firm?"

"I think the partners will understand. They loved Lavinia. Heck, half of them have, or had, kids at the school."

Audrey nodded. "Great. While you shower, I'll make breakfast."

He nodded. "By the way, when I called Harris to tell him Lavinia passed, I asked if he'd give the eulogy, and he agreed. I hope you don't mind."

"She would have wanted that. Thank you."

He kissed her gently and then rolled out of bed.

She waited until he was in the shower before steeling herself for the day. A prayer—that she could hold her tears in so as not to exacerbate their children's profound grief—gave her the strength she needed to rise from the bed, wrap her robe around herself, and head downstairs.

By the time Daniel came downstairs, the coffee had been brewed. Audrey put up the toast and began the task of cracking eggs to scramble. To her surprise, Charly, Chuck, and Noah entered the kitchen. Unlike her, they were dressed.

"It was perfectly alright for you to sleep in today," she reminded them.

Noah shook his head. "I really didn't sleep at all last night."

"Me neither," Chuck added. "Mom, we want to go with you."

Audrey's eyes shifted from Chuck to Charly. "That's sweet of you. But, really, it's not necessary."

"We know that," Charly assured her. "But she is…*was* our grandmother. We loved her too." Audrey understood Charly's reluctance for the past tense use of the endearment.

It's proof we've accepted she's gone.

"Wherever you need to be, we want to go with you," Noah insisted.

Audrey nodded reluctantly. "Lavinia should already be at the crematorium. After breakfast, we'll go to Lavinia's house. I need to pick out something to put her in for the cremation. The process should take a couple of hours, maybe three." She blinked away her tears. "You don't have to stay the whole time. Dad can take you to lunch."

Noah nodded slowly. "Will you be staying there?"

She nodded. "I think someone should."

Noah put his arms around his mother's waist. "Then we'll wait with you."

As Audrey kissed the top of his head, she caught Daniel's eye. There she saw a mix of sadness and appreciation.

Only Lavinia can make me feel this beloved.

Could make me feel.

She couldn't stifle her sobs at the realization that her mother would now always be thought of in the past tense.

When her family's arms embraced her, she thought she heard Lavinia whisper, *Always and forever.*

By the time Miranda had to leave for her lunch with Seamus, she'd tracked down five of her former Southern California concierge clients and got them to implicate themselves on the record by reiterating, and effusively at that, just how much they appreciated her illicit shenanigans on their behalf.

When SallyAnne told her to skip Tanner Simpson, Rob Edelson, and Eric Calisher, Miranda realized they'd been the clients who had flipped on her.

Two can play that game, she reasoned.

She was willing to guess that Eric, ever the hard-nosed businessman, would plead not guilty. As innocently as possible, she'd asked Lionel if this were the case.

He frowned. "When we confronted his wife, she committed suicide. And because the email account he used for his correspondence with you had only been accessed at their home and in her name, we have no way to tie him to an indictment."

She nodded slowly. "What if I gave you evidence that he was my sole contact?"

Lionel's eyes widened. "Our deal with him would be voided, and he'd be indicted."

"And it would count as one of my Girl Scout badges, right?"

Lionel sighed. "Yes, of course."

An hour later, she handed him a thumb drive. It contained the proof they needed: an audio file of Miranda's meeting with Eric, in which his son's rate was negotiated.

She hoped it bought her some of Lionel's respect, but she doubted it.

She guessed Tanner and Rob would plead guilty. When that happened, the reporter covering the story for the *Los Angeles Times* would receive the video of her and Rob making love.

For his betrayal, she owed him that much.

Those Miranda chose to call did not include the eight parents who had circled back to her this year with a second child whom they felt also needed her illicit help. After Winslow Jennings—the proctor she'd hired and set up at her fake testing subsidiary, University Prep & Test— disappeared on a gambling spree, he'd convinced her to abscond with their fees.

Miranda saw no need to let the Feds in on *that* little debacle. Why have grand theft added to her already long list of crimes?

These parents were on the list she'd turned in to the FBI. Eventually, she'd have to call them. By then, she prayed any deal her high-priced attorney made with them would be set in stone.

As she hung up from the final call, Lionel asked, "What kind of food do they serve at Zingari?"

"Expensive food." Miranda clicked her tongue in mock apology. "Probably off the charts when it comes to my FBI per diem. But it's one of Seamus' usual hangouts. I couldn't say no to him, now, could I?"

"There are food trucks on practically every corner of the Financial District," SallyAnne muttered.

Miranda chuckled, as if her nemesis had told a funny joke. "My clients don't do business with pikers."

Lionel still had the FBI-issued purse that Miranda had been instructed to use last night—one that had been customized with a video camera.

Miranda frowned when she saw it. Whereas yesterday she'd scoffed at its off-brand label, this time she shrugged. Picking up a compact, she pouted into the mirror as she ran a wand over her lips. "Am I to be on camera again?"

"Yes," Lionel replied firmly.

"That damn thing is black, and I'm wearing brown."

Lionel guffawed. "I'm sure Seamus won't even notice. He didn't strike me as a fashion maven."

Haughtily, she pulled out everything from her real purse and dumped it into the government-issued knock-off. Then, glancing at SallyAnne, she declared, "I suppose you'll be sitting this one out."

SallyAnne scoffed. "What gave you that idea?"

"Seamus knows what you look like." Miranda snapped the compact shut. "It's okay to wait in the van. Handsome can keep an eye on things." Her eyes studied Lionel from head to toe.

"Seamus saw Lionel too," SallyAnne reminded her.

Miranda shook her head. "I doubt he even noticed him.

He was too busy staring at your legs. Or hadn't you noticed?"

SallyAnne turned bright red.

"Thought so." Miranda's eyes widened, as if a thought had just occurred. "Perhaps you can make yourself useful by tailing Egan! But don't let him spot you. He's already smitten. Who knows what he'd do if he saw you?" Miranda smirked. "I guess I could say the same for you. You heard his performance, didn't you?"

SallyAnne had to purse her lips to hold herself back from cursing her out.

"Unless you think it's a bad idea." She slid her gaze to Lionel, as if the decision were his to make.

Lionel's face was impassive. Still, SallyAnne guessed what he might be thinking: Miranda had a point. Seamus might indeed remember her. And if Melamed was able to fast-track Egan's surveillance subpoena, having SallyAnne review the calls, emails, and texts monitored by Riley's team might not be a bad idea—

Despite Lionel's personal preference that she stay away from Egan.

Lionel's nonchalant shrug was proof that SallyAnne had guessed right: he thought Miranda had a point.

As Miranda tucked the compact into her purse, she asked, "Agent Polk, since you're tailing me anyway, wouldn't it make sense that we ride over together? That way your *partner*"—she lingered on the word a second too long—"can take the car back to the office." Seeing his surprise, she added, "It was just a thought. Not to worry. I'd return you in one piece."

SallyAnne saw no need to wait for his response. She walked out without a word.

At Lionel's insistence, they arrived a good twenty minutes before the scheduled meeting, which gave them plenty of time to park in a nearby garage and secure tables close enough that he could video record her.

Miranda went ahead and ordered a bottle of wine. She knew Seamus would expect it, and besides, she needed a drink after the past forty-eight hours. Had it been that long since she'd first been arrested?

Jeez, it seems like a lifetime, she thought.

Seamus came ten minutes late—plenty of time for her to drink half the waiter's generous pour of a very expensive cabernet sauvignon.

Jess Smallwood and Warner Crawford were with him.

Oh, bloody hell.

Miranda caught Lionel's eyes opening wide at the sight of Seamus' entourage.

Seamus chuckled as he squeezed into the booth on one side of her, confident in his supposedly secret mission.

Miranda would hear it soon enough.

"A shame about Lavinia." Jess also slid into the booth on Miranda's other side. He thought nothing of squeezing her thigh under the table.

Miranda was tempted to dig her nail into the back of his hand. But his yelp would alert the other men as to what had just happened. Instead, she murmured, "Yes, isn't it?"

If Jess truly wants to sound sincere, he should take that shit-eating grin off his face, she thought.

"I guess AA will now go into the crapper," Warner fretted. "The kids really liked her. Even my son, Buck, minded his P's and Q's around her."

"Not to worry," Seamus huffed. "The new Head of School will keep him in line."

A new head of school…

Oh, bother.

Seamus' big plan was to fast-track some new administrator!

If the new schoolmaster were power-hungry (and most were, Miranda reasoned; seriously, who wouldn't get a high lording it over a teaching staff, a bunch of sniveling students, and fawning parents who considered themselves lucky to be one of such a highly regarded school's chosen few?), she could find herself sidelined from any activities that took her outside those she'd committed to the school.

Which means she'd have less leverage with the FBI.

I've got to make sure the trustee board draws out the search as long as possible.

"She is irreplaceable indeed," Miranda declared. "That being said, I would hope that the trustee board takes its time in finding someone who comes close to filling her shoes—"

"To hell with that!" Seamus bellowed. "We're going to fill it immediately—and permanently. In fact, I've got just the candidate."

"Mustn't be too hasty," Miranda cautioned. "We may end up with another bleeding heart do-gooder."

Seamus raised a brow. "I doubt that very much"—he poured wine into his glass, then raised it toward her. He waited until she raised hers too, then declared—"since it'll be *you*."

What…

Oh, hell!

Miranda almost dropped her glass. "What? I can't! ... *I won't—*"

Not in a million years.

"Sure you will," Seamus growled. "We put you on the board for one reason: to assure it lives up to our standards." He shrugged. "Quit worrying."

She could see it now. As the FBI dragged Miranda away in handcuffs, the parents would fight them off, if only for the honor of stringing her up from the bell tower.

I will have ruined their children's futures. Even those whose kids weren't involved will know the school will be tarnished by the scandal.

I have to nip this in the bud—NOW.

"As honored as I am by your confidence, I don't feel it would be a good fit," Miranda insisted. "You forget, Seamus. Beyond my current obligation to Ashbury Academy, I've got a private practice as well."

She picked up the purse and rose from her seat. As far as she was concerned, the topic was closed.

Seamus put his hand on her arm. "Believe me, Miranda. Our interests are well aligned."

She frowned. "How so?"

He tugged her back down into her chair. "As headmistress, you are perfectly positioned to recruit new parents to the school whose philosophy aligns with Warner's, Jess', and mine. Parents who would do anything—*and pay anything*—to get into the universities of their choice." He leaned in so close that she could smell his breath. "Miranda, imagine a whole school willing to pay your fee —all because you've guaranteed getting their kids into the universities of their choice!"

Miranda's glare shifted from Seamus to Jess to Warner

and back again. "I think you're forgetting, Seamus. Our arrangement was *strictly confidential.*"

Seamus chuckled. "Quit being so paranoid! You don't have to worry about Warner here. He's the client referral I mentioned. Trust me, he's all in!"

He jutted his chin toward Warner, who nodded vigorously.

She set the purse back onto the table, the clasp turned toward Warner, so that its camera saw him fully. "What you're telling me, Mr. Crawford, is that you don't mind in the least that my college admissions concierge program may include some illicit acts?"

Warner guffawed. "Buck is the laziest kid at the school. And no matter how many times I've warned him that he can't just send a headshot to get into the school of his choice, he insists he can just skirt by on his looks." He sighed mightily, proof he was resigned to this fact. "So yeah, I'm in. Otherwise, my retirement fund will go to supporting a spendthrift party animal for the rest of his life."

Seamus jabbed Miranda's arm. "See? What did I tell you? He's all in! In fact, he knows at least two other parents who are just as anxious to get their kids into one of their top school picks."

As long as Seamus and his friends were doing the hard work, why not just lean back and enjoy the ride?

Lean back, she did. "Are you suggesting that we build my fee—including the pass-along costs—into the tuition?"

"Eventually, yes," Jess replied. "After this year, like their children, parents will be vetted differently—*to see if they're a good fit with the school's new philosophy.*"

The more desperate, the better, Miranda thought.

"We have two legacies on the current trustee board, a

high-profile member who was Lavinia's closest and dearest friend, and another board member who is married to Lavinia's daughter. How do you think they'll feel about this?"

"They'll hate it. Maybe so much that they'll quit the board." Seamus smiled at the thought. "Look, Miranda, if I don't go in asking for the whole hog, they won't even settle for giving me the tail, let alone the squeal. Let me play hardball. Interim Head will be our fallback position."

"Works for me," she murmured.

Prayerfully, the search would go on long enough that she'd never have the title permanently, and with it the wrath of the Ashbury Academy community.

"Once you're installed as Interim Head of School, you'll be tasked with heading up the New Family Acceptance Committee."

Miranda nodded. "My criterion is simple: anyone who is desperate enough to contribute, minimally half a million dollars per student, will automatically be enrolled in the concierge program."

Warner sputtered on his wine. "You want me to cough up *half a mil*?"

"Hardly! As you've just admitted, Buck is dumb as a post. That warrants a fee of *a million dollars*." Miranda turned to Seamus. "Which brings us to what I'll expect for the salary as Head of School." She leaned in. "If minimally, I'm to work my magic for six more students next year, I'll need an additional three million."

Seamus shrugged. "And for a whole graduating class?"

Miranda took a moment to think. Finally, she declared, "Each successive year, my salary will be predicated on the number of new families who are accepted due to the change in our mission. By the fifth year, the salary will be…oh, say, twenty million."

Jess smirked. "That should fatten the quote unquote 'endowment fund.'"

"Tuition will be raised too," she warned.

Jess frowned. He was thinking of his daughter from his second wife, who would graduate in three years.

"Look at it this way. It's a pittance as to what I'd charge them individually," Miranda countered. "These assurances don't come cheap, you know. Not to mention each *new* family's fee is spread over the four years their child is in school. And besides, the parents who fit our philosophy will be able to afford the increases." She shrugged. "I know you well enough to figure out you are looking for a deal and want to spread the investment. Well, those are my terms, gentlemen. Take it or leave it."

The men exchanged glances. Finally, Seamus growled, "Done—with one exception." He puffed up. "Until the school is at a point where every parent has bought into this new programming feature, those who have done so will prove it by their donations to the newly established 'Lavinia Thorpe Memorial Endowment Fund.'"

Knowing him, it'll be anything but, Miranda realized.

Still, she murmured, "And let me guess who will be controlling this fund—you. Am I right?"

Seamus shrugged. "I'd be honored to increase its corpus with sound investments."

Miranda's laugh rang through the restaurant. "My God, Seamus! You're shameless!" Studying her nails, she added, "Do me a favor and save the motion until after Lavinia's funeral. That way, you don't look like a complete Machiavellian overlord. Besides, we don't need a civil war breaking out."

Seamus scowled, then nodded grudgingly. He raised his glass to her. "Here's to Ashbury Academy finally becoming the school worth our investment."

"I'll drink to that," Jess declared.

As he picked up his glass, Miranda glanced directly at Lionel and winked.

I should get a medal for this—right, Handsome?

Instead, I'll end up in some cell—one I'll probably share with Gretchen McCoppin.

Maybe that wouldn't be so bad. At least, there would be no question who'd be the alpha in that relationship.

As previously instructed by Lionel, Miranda allowed the men to leave first.

Jess tried to linger, but his suggestion of some "afternoon delight" was met with a harried sigh.

"My afternoon is booked with client appointments. And by the way, from what we've just discussed about my fees, maybe you should be shaking your magic money tree so that you're not so stretched by the time your daughter, Elowen, is in her senior year. Last I heard, she's got her eye on Yale."

Jess turned white, mumbled some vague answer, and then did as he was told.

"What a dolt," Miranda muttered.

That was for Lionel's sake.

Lionel followed a few yards behind Miranda until they reached the garage.

Instead of dropping her off at her apartment, he drove straight to FBI headquarters, where SallyAnne, Riley, and Director Melamed were waiting for them in one of the conference rooms.

Miranda smirked. "Wow, what a welcoming committee! I guess I did well."

"Behave yourself, Miranda." The disemboweled voice of her attorney, Gerald Breslin, came in over the speaker on the conference room table. "Seamus' scheme moves this investigation into a whole different league. We can add money laundering to the list of indictments."

Riley started counting them off on his fingers: "Bribery, racketeering, criminal conspiracy, honest services mail fraud—"

"I get the picture," Miranda retorted. "I'll do it—but only if it means I walk without jail time."

"That depends on how successful his scheme is," Melamed countered. "I seriously doubt he has the votes to make this happen."

Miranda shrugged. "We'll see about that." Egan was still her ace in the hole. Metaphorically speaking, anyway.

"By the way, you've just received a text from Daniel McKittridge," Riley declared. "The memorial service is being held at the school on Wednesday, at eleven o'clock."

Miranda glared at him. "You're a wonderful private secretary. Did you RSVP for me as well?"

"Yeah," he admitted. "I mean, I knew you'd want to attend…"

His voice faded when he realized Melamed was glowering at him.

"We'll be your ride to the memorial service," Lionel added.

Miranda frowned. "Why do I need an entourage? It's

not like I'll be hustling parents while everyone is bawling over Lavinia."

"Seamus has no filter," Lionel pointed out. "And now he has a vested interest in you. He may actually recruit a few other parents during the service and walk them over to you at some point."

She couldn't argue with that.

"We'll be discreet, so no need to worry. Unless you're going with your boyfriend—*Egan*." SallyAnne's remark had Miranda flinching—proof it had hit its mark like a poison dart.

Lionel's brow rose in consternation.

Ignoring him, SallyAnne paused, as if a thought just came to her. "Oh, wait…he broke up with you, didn't he?"

Miranda stiffened. "As far as you're concerned, Egan is serving his purpose."

"As long as you keep him in play," Melamed reminded her. "Otherwise, you'll never be able to deliver on your promise."

"He cashed the check, didn't he? Then he's in play," Miranda huffed. "Although, I'll admit having sex with him was a mistake."

"So sorry it didn't work out, since you obviously enjoyed it," SallyAnne murmured.

Lionel shot her a look that was meant to silence her, but it was too late.

Miranda scowled at SallyAnne. "Oh yes, I forgot—the FBI is now my constant companion." She shrugged as if to say, *so be it.* "If you really want to get up close and personal, you should attend as my date," she cooed to Lionel.

"He may run into Egan—who may remember him." SallyAnne countered.

"I doubt it," Miranda muttered. "He only had eyes for you."

SallyAnne's cheeks pinked up.

Miranda's attention shifted to Lionel. "Don't you agree?"

SallyAnne knew Miranda's game: divide and conquer.

But proof Lionel wasn't falling for it was his reply: "Of course I do. We're all going—Riley included."

"But…" Miranda's jaw jutted out in anger. "No one in Lavinia's circle knows you. You'll stick out like sore thumbs."

"It'll be a large crowd—easy for us to blend in. It's what we do for a living," he reminded her. "If you're that concerned, we'll put on disguises. Look, here's the thing, Miranda: until the indictments are served, we're going to be on you like white on rice. Get used to it."

The message was clear: he didn't trust her.

She could live with that—at least until she was free of the FBI.

CHAPTER 5

The public Celebration of Life for Lavinia was to take place at the school on Wednesday at eleven. As was her wish, at dawn, Audrey, Daniel, and the children spread her ashes off Fort Point, below the Golden Gate Bridge in a private memorial ceremony.

They were joined by those who knew Lavinia best: Bliss and her parents, Reggie and Maude Thackeray, as well as her husband, Raffaele, and their daughter, Sienna. Tallulah was also there, with her husband and son, Jammerhead and Quest. Her mother, Maggie, sobbed inconsolably. Lavinia had been her oldest and dearest friend and confidante.

Davis had also shown up.

Harris was there too, although his wife, Tracy, was still in Washington, having committed to head the fundraiser for a national charity.

Each took a teaspoon of Lavinia's sifted ashes before saying a few words about the woman who had touched their lives so profoundly. They then released the ashes into the frigid, fast-flowing current which marks where the turbulent Pacific Ocean meets the calm wake of San Francisco Bay.

Audrey took her turn last. She did so without saying a word. There were too many things she wished she had said to her mother when she was alive. Too many questions she wished she'd asked.

Would Lavinia have answered?

Now she'd never know.

Clare had insisted that Audrey delegate the set-up of the event to her and the teaching staff. By the time the McKittridges arrived, a stage had been placed in the center of the quad.

Rows of white chairs stretched out from it, like the spokes on a wheel. Hanging from the trees throughout the park were laminated poster-sized photos of Lavinia: with staff, students, and parents, tracing her life at the school. Each image had been selected and signed by a student.

As it should be, Audrey thought. *The school was no less a part of her life than me.*

Immediately, Audrey and her family were wrapped in consoling hugs by mourners. Grief was etched deeply into their faces.

Audrey tried to respond to their gently murmured condolences, but the words stuck in her throat.

Lavinia was always the one to console others, Audrey thought. *She always knew the right thing to say.*

I'll never be like her.

I don't have her strength of character.

As if reading her mind, Daniel whispered into her ear, "I'll speak for the family, if you want."

Relieved, Audrey nodded. She took Daniel's hand. He led her to the front row seats reserved for them.

<hr>

It was fitting that Harris, Lavinia's oldest and closest friend, deliver her eulogy.

Through his candor, the students who dearly missed the headmistress were introduced to a much younger Lavinia. One who questioned her professors at Berkeley with the verve of a prosecuting attorney. Who never thought twice of inviting down-on-their-luck friends to crash on her couch. And whose Sunday open houses were more fondly recalled for her homemade soups and bread than for the dreams, schemes, and political discourse espoused by the multitude of students in attendance.

Quite a few Ashbury Academy parents teared up when Harris recalled the day Lavinia told him why she was determined to start her own school after spending almost fifteen years teaching, both in private and public institutions: "'The greatest joy is the students,' she explained. 'But despite what anyone says, the administrative vision isn't *student-driven*. If it's not controlled by a union, it is micromanaged by parents. That should never be! The students show us what they need. We must guide them to reach their and society's goals. This school will do just that.'"

The parents in the audience nodded even as they laughed uncomfortably. They saw themselves in her declaration.

After leaving the stage, Harris walked through the

crowd. Arms reached out to him with hands ready to shake or grasp him in appreciation for his touching words.

SallyAnne and the rest of her team were scattered within the crowd. She'd always liked Harris as her Congressman. But now, for the first time, she appreciated him as just another person.

Because Miranda was wired, the agents could hear her mutter, "Bravo, Harris! Looks like you locked up a few more votes and donors."

What a bitch, SallyAnne thought.

Clare rushed onto the stage. But by the way the school's sweet but shy receptionist shook, it was evident she was nervous about being there.

In her palm, she held a smooth rock: one of the many that were placed throughout the campus' flower beds. Her voice was so soft that the crowd leaned in to hear what she had to say. "As most of you are aware, Ashbury Academy has a tradition: it's called 'magic circle.'"

Waves of knowing nods rippled through the crowd. "By passing around a river rock, we are encouraged to speak up and talk through our feelings when the rock comes our way. Lavinia felt that honest conversation was a path to resolution." Clare wiped away her tears with the back of her hand. Her voice cracked as she added, "I know we won't resolve our grief, but it may help us process it."

Taking the hand-held microphone with her, she left the stage. She handed the rock to the first person she saw—a junior student, a boy—while holding the mic for him.

Jesus, I never felt that way about a teacher, let alone a principal, Riley thought.

Thus far, six mourners had reached out for the river rock and spoke from their hearts about the revered headmistress. Three had been students, two were parents, and one was the seemingly ancient French teacher—she'd given her name as Odette Pettigrew—who had been with the school since the day it opened.

As Madame Pettigrew's voice rose and fell dramatically, Riley stared up at the school's clock tower. He couldn't help but envision this none-too-beauteous Schéhérazade as a gargoyle perched on the peak of its witches' cap roof.

Admittedly, each mourner's memory of Lavinia had been more touching than the last.

The girl speaking now sat across the aisle from him. In a halting voice, she recalled fretting over an oral book report. As she passed Lavinia on her way to class, the headmistress intuitively sensed her anxiety.

In no time, she got the girl to divulge her fear.

"Lavinia suggested I imagine talking to my best friends about the book. That I summarize the story and then tell them all the things I loved about it, but also the things that didn't ring true." The girl smiled. "It worked! I got an A! I was so happy that I stopped into Lavinia's office later that day to tell her about it. She hugged me and said, 'I knew you'd do well. Only we can hold ourselves back from accomplishing our goals.'" The girl's eyes grew misty. "I can still hear her voice in my mind. Can't we all? Because what she said to us resonates in our hearts." As if weighted down with her sorrow, the girl's head dropped to her chest. "She lives on through all of us."

Everyone seemed to be wiping away their tears. Those

around the girl comforted her with pats on the back. The ensuing silence was filled with the sobs of a few mourners unable to contain their grief.

Suddenly realizing she still held the river rock, the embarrassed girl thrust it toward Riley.

Shit! … SHIT! What do I do now?

Like all FBI agents, he'd been trained to be as unobtrusive as possible. He was there to observe, not to participate.

But now all eyes were on him.

To his horror, Clare stuck the microphone in his face.

Riley was the center of attention.

"I…. I…" the stammer was to buy time; to think through how he could blend in.

As if.

"I was only here a short time. Not even a semester," he murmured.

A strangled voice, somewhere from another side of the campus, yelled, "Louder, please!"

Riley nodded. In a stronger voice, he added, "Every day, I'd come home, in awe of my classmates, my teachers —and of course, Lavinia."

He buried his head in his hands. *Stall…. STALL.*

Finally, he let out a long sigh. "Still, I didn't feel as if I belonged there…I mean *here*."

Watch it. You're blowing your cover!

"I was sitting by myself—on that bench over there, in fact—when she walked past me. It was as if she knew the turmoil I was feeling. She sat right down beside me and asked, 'How are you?' And it all came out! All my anxieties, my fears. My hurt."

Those closest to him reached out to touch his arm, encouraging him to continue.

Ah, hell.

"She was so...*so kind!* Insightful. And inspiring!" he continued. "She told me I could be anything I wanted, that I could do anything I set my mind to." He dropped his head. "And she was right. In fact, that night, I informed my parents that when I graduated, I wanted to go to...*to mime school.*"

A murmur went through the crowd

Shit! Was that too unbelievable? Say something that sounds real—now!

"They were so upset that they pulled me out of school. They'd decided the school was too...well, in their words, 'too liberal'"—

The mourners gasped.

"—which is why none of you remember me." He didn't know if that was a great cover, but it was all he could think of. "It's why I'm here now. Because of Lavinia, I became the best mime in...err...*Bolivia!* There, I'm known as 'the Mime King.'" He laughed weakly. "Or as they say in my new country, '*El Rey Memo.*'" For once, Riley was glad his high school Spanish paid off.

Elated, he wiped away a tear of relief.

Suddenly, he was enveloped in hugs.

Wow...this feels AWESOME...

Egan had been standing in the back of the campus, behind

all the chairs. He'd seen Audrey come in with her family, only to be swallowed up in the crowd.

After our meeting the night of Lavinia's death, the last person she wants to see now is me, he realized.

Miranda was also there. Luckily, the crowd was thick enough that he'd succeeded in ducking out of view whenever she glanced in his direction.

Right now, everyone's eyes were on the goober, whose tale about Lavinia had turned the celebration of her life into a big cryfest.

Egan dove through the crowd until he was at Clare's side. Pointing to the sobbing stranger, he hissed, "We've got to do something, Clare! The crowd is drowning in its own tears! Go up there! Say something that's *uplifting!*"

Clare's eyes grew large with fear. With a shaky whisper, she pleaded, "I—I can't! Please, Egan, do it for me...*for her!*"

He knew she meant Lavinia. Still, instinctively, his eyes went to Audrey. She was crying harder than anyone. Daniel leaned over her helplessly, trying to comfort her.

Egan frowned. "You knew Lavinia the longest! Wouldn't it be better coming from you?"

Clare shook her head, adamantly. "No—please*! I don't like speaking in public.* I'm a behind-the-scenes person. And for you—it comes so naturally!"

Egan nodded, but he wasn't happy about it.

He stooped down and picked up another of the palm-sized stones.

This one's for you, Lavinia.

CHAPTER 6

*E*gan leaped up onto the stage, holding the stone high.

"My name is Egan Gable, and I teach Comparative Literature here at Ashbury Academy." He nodded to the crowd. "I, like you, am here because Lavinia Thorpe touched my life. I'll go further and say she was such a force of nature that she changed the fate of many—me included. I'd like to share the one act that impacted me the most."

Egan looked down at the mourners, all the while steeling himself from the natural inclination to look at Audrey. "It was the day I met her. The school was entering its fourth year. I told her I was a thesis candidate at Berkeley in Creative Writing. That was true—but barely. In fact, I'd just gotten word that the committee considered my thesis—a novel—mediocre at best. To top it off, my parents made it abundantly clear that they weren't going to support me financially as I wrote my version of the great

American novel in various and sundry New York coffee shops—"

He got a chuckle with that remark.

"—so, I needed a job and fast." Egan sighed. "As fate would have it, Ashbury Academy needed an English teacher. And *voila!* —a match was made in heaven." Letting loose with a broad grin, he looked skyward but then shook his head. "I wish I could say it was that easy, but we all know Lavinia much better than that. No way was she going to entrust her precious students to *just anyone.*"

Throughout the crowd, heads bobbed. Giggles filled the air.

"Instead," he continued, "she wants to know *everything* about you. Not the just the stuff you think she wants to hear, either—*but the stuff you really don't ever want anyone to know.*"

By now, the chuckles were outright guffaws.

"She wanted to know where I'd grown up. And what I'd done for fun as a kid. And the most important lessons my parents had taught me." He let that sink in. "She wanted to know why I chose to be a Lit major, and if there were anything I'd change about my academic journey."

The crowd froze, enthralled.

"So, of course, I lied."

Now the crowd was laughing outright.

"I created the backstory I wished I had lived, minimizing my heartache and failures. I did so because I was sure she'd think worse of me had she heard the truth, never realizing—at least, not yet—that one of Lavinia's hidden talents was that she could read minds. And that her ex-ray vision easily pierced the armor our egos forged from the tiny fibs we must tell ourselves to hold up our heads; simply to survive another day."

His audience nodded as if seeing themselves through his tale.

"So, no, I didn't fool her. Not in the least. And yet, she chose to see the best in me." Egan looked skyward as if seeing his friend and mentor there. "I had a pancake-flat vision of myself. But like some great chef, Lavinia added those few missing ingredients—a dollop of inspiration, a sprinkle of kindness, and heaps of responsibility garnished with just enough accountability to make me realize my potential—and turned it into the flavorful, satisfying soufflé that is my life." He paused. "We are all fortunate to have had her in our lives." He paused, then added, "But no one knows that better than her family."

He pointed to the McKittridges—

To Audrey, specifically.

He loved Lavinia too.

Audrey saw that immediately.

And he is right. Lavinia saw right through him.

This realization caused her to laugh through her tears.

She saw through me too. She knew I'd been infatuated with him.

But it didn't matter. Lavinia let fate take its course.

At that moment, her mother's final words came to her: *Tell Daniel about Egan.*

It had been almost a week since her mother's death—plenty of time to try to convince herself that she'd misheard Lavinia.

But she knew better. Somehow, Lavinia had deduced

the secret Audrey had kept for eighteen years: that the twins' father was Egan.

All that time, Audrey had lived with the shame of keeping her secret from Daniel.

Oh, how Audrey wished she could have convinced herself that Lavinia's declaration was murmured through a fog of delusion! But no. Even as Death beckoned her forward, Lavinia had summoned the energy to open her eyes one last time.

They say that the eyes are the windows to the soul, Audrey thought. Her mother's last clear-eyed gaze had put all doubts to rest.

I can't tell Daniel yet.

The thought that day would eventually come had her suddenly sobbing uncontrollably.

Daniel put his arm around her and whispered, "Honey, are you alright?"

At that moment, she realized that Egan had stopped talking and that his arm was held out to her.

Why? What had he just said?

Daniel, too, must have realized she'd just been singled out because his back stiffened. "Do you want to say something?"

She shook her head. "*No!* I can't ...not now—"

He patted her hand. "I'll speak for the family then."

Daniel rose and walked to the stage.

"He's such a blowhard."

Seamus had sidled so closely to Miranda that his breath felt warm on her neck.

Still, he'd said it loud enough that several mourners glanced over, shaking their heads in dismay.

He then tapped her arm with something—an envelope.

She stared down at it. "Is that what I think it is?"

"What do you think it is?" Seamus smiled supremely. "It's your pay-off for fixing my beautiful-but-dumb daughter's SAT test."

She glowered at him. "You fool! You were supposed to make an electronic funds transfer to The Best Face Forward Club!" she said in a hush.

Seamus' face fell. "What the hell does it matter?"

"It matters a lot, you dolt! It makes the transaction a legitimate donation!" she shoved the envelope at his chest. *"Just do it."*

Mollified, he slunk back into the crowd.

She didn't realize Lionel was right behind her until he muttered: "It wasn't necessary. We could take it and pull his fingerprints off the bills to make our case."

Miranda didn't turn around but growled, "I wanted to kick his ass. I don't need him cutting corners and screwing up my deal with you."

"Good point."

Then, silence.

She didn't need to turn around to know Lionel had already slipped away.

Beautiful but dumb daughter?

He's paying her to fake my test?

Why that son of a bitch!

Neither Miranda nor Seamus had realized Fawn was standing right there behind them—

Close enough to hear how little he thought of her.

He doesn't believe I can get admitted to college on my own—let alone get accepted by his hoity-toity alma mater, Yale.

Great. Fine. No surprise there.

Seamus may have changed the rules of the game, but she could still win: by raking in as many acceptances as possible—

And then turning them all down.

Including Yale.

Game on, she vowed.

Like Egan, Daniel chose an uplifting anecdote.

And like the rest of the crowd, Egan had been listening to Daniel, which is why it took him a while to realize that someone had moved beside him.

He gave the man a sidelong glance, taking note that he was younger. He was also vaguely familiar.

As if reading his mind, the man said, "Egan, it's me—Davis Wong. Long time, no see."

Egan did a doubletake. Yes, the face was the same, but now that he was thirty-nine—forty, perhaps—there were a few lines around his eyes and his forehead. Although his torso was still slight, he'd bulked up, but in a good way.

He held out his hand. "It's great to see you, Davis."

Taking it, Davis declared, "I have to tell you, *Extracurricular* was a great book. I read it when it first came out."

"Why, thank you." Taken aback, Egan shrugged. "And it's been wonderful following your success in LaLa Land."

Davis chuckled. "Maybe I can spread some of my fame and fortune your way. In fact, recently, I picked up *Extracurricular* again. I loved it even more. Laughed in all the right places, cried in a couple too." Davis hesitated. "In fact, I'd like to option it for a television series."

Egan's heart seemed to leap in his chest. "I'm...flattered, to say the least. More so because it's you." He hesitated. "I hate to sound so ignorant about your industry, but tell me: what does this mean in monetary terms?"

"There will be option money, in the mid to high six figures. And if a network wants it, that will double the option I've paid for. If it goes to pilot, even more." Davis shrugged. "Or it could go straight to series, and that's when the big payoff happens."

Egan's eyes grew wide. "Big? What are we talking about?"

"Depends on the terms that your agent can get."

Egan frowned. "I don't know if my lit agent has my back. The publisher recently pulled it from publication because of a lawsuit."

Davis shook his head, awed. "Jesus! Whatever for?"

Egan sighed. "Remember Mandy Blackwell? She rightly guessed the character based on her and threw a lawsuit at me. 'Defamation of character.'"

Davis snorted. "Frankly, I thought what you wrote was a love letter. Ah, well, no accounting for taste." He looked around. "I don't see her here. But the crowd is pretty thick, and it has been over twenty years."

Egan looked skyward. "Don't remind me."

Davis patted his shoulder. "You look great—for an old man."

Egan laughed.

Suddenly, he remembered where he was and pursed his lips. He need not have bothered. Everyone around them was suddenly talking and moving. A few were also laughing. Apparently, Daniel had brought the proceedings to a close on a high note.

Thank goodness, Egan thought.

At that moment, he realized Audrey was staring at him.

Bliss and Tallulah were beside her.

Davis must have noticed, too, because he declared, "My sweet, sweet Audrey." Without a second thought, he waved them over.

Audrey hesitated, grimacing.

She doesn't want to come over because of me.

But a moment later they were at his side.

CHAPTER 7

"Hi, Doll. How are you holding up?" Watching as Davis kissed Audrey's cheek gently, Egan yearned to do the same.

Her lips rose unsteadily into a treacly smile. "I'm okay. The kids …it's a big blow to them."

More so because they hadn't known how ill Lavinia was, Egan reasoned.

Audrey held out her hand to Egan. "Thank you for those very kind words about Lavinia. And for lifting everyone's spirits." She managed a weak smile.

Tallulah craned her head for a better look at Riley. "Who was that mime guy anyway?"

"I didn't recognize him," Audrey admitted. "Although he couldn't have been that much younger than us. And although we had a few students come in mid-year, I certainly don't remember anyone leaving in the middle of the school year, or for that matter, parents being angry at Lavinia for being too progressive. It's what you buy into at AA."

Bliss raised a brow. "Well, at least the dude got into the school of his choice."

Egan snickered. "I've got to write that into a novel."

Davis turned to him. "Speaking of novels, if you're interested in my offer for *Extracurricular*, I can recommend a couple of talent agencies that have literary divisions and might represent you in the deal. Neither reps me, so they'd have, as they say, clean hands."

Egan felt his cheeks flaring. He hadn't expected Davis to bring up their conversation in front of anyone there, let alone Audrey.

"You want to produce *Extracurricular* as a movie?" Bliss asked.

"No," Egan said quickly.

"A TV adaptation," Davis explained.

Egan noticed that all the color drained from Audrey's face.

"Ha! Yeah, now that you mention it, I could see that," Tallulah exclaimed. "It's got that whole *This is Us* vibe going for it! You know, retro and touchy-feely at the same time."

"More like *Clueless*," Audrey muttered as she glowered at Egan.

"Except that it's got that great love story," Bliss pointed out. She looked sideways at Egan. "Although, for the life of me, I can't understand why you based your protagonist on Mandy Blackwell, of all people!"

"*Mandy?*" Egan couldn't believe his ears. He was about to set her straight, but he felt a jab to his back and he turned around.

It was Audrey. Her glare warned him to hold his tongue.

She's right, he thought. Better they should assume it was Mandy than Audrey.

"I don't know who you'd get to play me," Tallulah continued. "...Oh, wait! Maybe Kate Hudson. She married a musician, so she knows the life."

"No model-actress will play me," Bliss warned Davis, "unless I play myself."

"Okay! I promise! There's this new CGI that allows us to make you look twenty years younger. So, yeah, I think we can pull that off." He raised his hands to his face as if buffering any blows that may come his way.

"How about you, Audrey? Who would you want to see…" Tallulah turned, only to find that her old friend was gone.

Egan caught sight of Audrey disappearing into the crowd.

If I let Davis option it, she'll hate me.

But by doing so, I can get out from under Miranda's thumb once and for all.

"I think Daniel waved her over," Egan lied. Nodding to Davis, Bliss, and Tallulah, he added, "In fact, I think Clare needs me. Please excuse me."

He set out after Audrey.

Egan roamed through the throng of mourners until he found Audrey. She was sitting alone on a bench. It was in an alcove that, miraculously, had not been overtaken by some of the other mourners milling close by.

As he approached, Audrey shook her head as if to say, *please leave me alone.*

Instead, he sat down beside her.

"I didn't broach the idea of bringing *Extracurricular* to the screen with Davis. I swear!"

Audrey sighed. "I believe it. When we told Davis you were teaching here again, he made it clear he'd been impressed by your book."

He snickered. "Who are 'we'?"

"Tallulah and Bliss...and me." Audrey blushed. "They knew he'd be interested in the fact that you're back at AA."

Egan grinned. "I guess I should be flattered that I merited the call."

"Yeah, well, believe me—it wasn't my idea. I knew it would dredge up *Extracurricular.*" She looked down at her hands. "They will guess, Egan! My children—*my husband* —will know you were in love with me! And I'm sure Daniel will put two and two together about...the timeline of it all."

As he watched a tear roll off her cheek and fall into her lap, the crack he felt in his heart now seemed a vast crevice. "I want you to know this, Audrey. If I say yes— and that's a really *big* if—it's because—"

"Egan!"

Recognizing the voice, Egan shut up. Out of the corner of his eye, he saw Charly trotting toward him.

She had Noah with her.

The boy was the spitting image of Daniel. Now, knowing what he did about Chuck and Charly, Egan wondered how obvious the twins' resemblance to him might be to others when they stood next to him.

Would Daniel one day see the resemblance?

A part of him wished he would.

But no, it'll never happen, he reasoned. When Daniel looks at the twins, he sees them through eyes brimming with love, pride, and devotion.

We only see what we want.

"Egan!" Charly shocked him when she threw her arms around him in a tight hug. "I was so touched with what you said about Lavinia."

"I...I loved your grandmother." He said it to Charly, but his gaze took in Noah too.

Charly attempted a smile through quivering lips. "Have you met my brother, Noah?"

Egan patted the boy's shoulder. "Nice to meet you finally."

Noah scrutinized Egan with one eye shut. "You taught Mom too?"

"Yes. She was my favorite student."

Audrey frowned at the compliment.

Charly snickered. "You mean until you had *me*."

"You've certainly come in a close second—*thus far,*" Egan warned her. "Your mom is a hard act to follow." He glanced over at Audrey. "Listen, would you mind if your mom and I took a moment to—"

"Ah, here you all are!"

The sound of Miranda's voice made Egan flinch. He turned to find her behind him.

Daniel was with her.

Chuck was with them too, and he was grinning from ear to ear. As he gave Egan a quick hug, he exclaimed, "Wow, you said some pretty great things about Lavinia! I guess you couldn't fool her either."

Egan laughed. "By that, I take it you tried yourself a few times?"

Chuck nodded. "Yep. She saw right through me too." His voice grew softer as he added, "I want to be more like her."

"We all do," Audrey murmured.

As they stood silently with that thought, Egan glanced over at Miranda. She'd managed a placid smile. She'd also made it a point to avoid looking at him.

Fine with me.

"With that in mind, I've followed up on Dad's suggestion to use Miranda's help with my college submissions." Chuck nodded toward the college counselor. "In fact, she's placing me in her concierge program!"

Miranda took Audrey's hand. "I'm so glad Daniel suggested it. I'd already reviewed Chuck's grades and his teachers' notes on his study habits, and I was concerned he was showing signs of ADHD or some other learning disability. With Daniel's approval—and yours too, of course—we start our assessment as soon as possible."

"If he's agreeable, then yes, by all means..." Audrey's voice trailed off. Consternation was etched on her brow.

Egan couldn't believe his ears: *Miranda had convinced Daniel to pay for Chuck's test to be forged.*

"Not to worry," Miranda assured her. "Even if it turns out I'm right, Chuck will be able to take the test privately and untimed—with AA's teacher proctor, of course," Miranda continued.

Chuck slapped Egan on the back. "Miranda mentioned you volunteered to coach those in the program and be its test proctor too."

"Did she, now?" Egan hoped they hadn't picked up on the edge in his voice. His eyes moved to Miranda.

But before he could say anything, Miranda added, "I'm so appreciative that Egan leaped at the opportunity! I'm sure he'll work it around your other activities—Debate Team, basketball, whatnot. But we don't have much time. The final test takes place just a few weeks away—the last Saturday in November."

"Well, then, we'd better get cracking," Daniel said. "Whatever assignments Egan gives you in preparation for it, you'll be on top of it, right?"

Chuck nodded. "I'll do my best."

I'm supposed to help my son cheat just because his so-called father doesn't believe in him.

Just the thought of it made Egan sick to his gut.

Lovingly, Daniel put his arm around Audrey's waist.

She leaned into him, then turned up her face.

He kissed her on the lips.

As Egan looked away, he caught Miranda's eye. Beaming, she had the audacity to wink at him.

He quelled the urge to slap her. Instead, he walked away.

The woman looked familiar—

Well, sort of.

The hair was different: longer, and blonde.

But she was petite. And those beautiful dark almond-shaped eyes. Even her glasses couldn't hide the gentle intent he found in them.

Yes, she was staring right at him.

Intrigued, Egan walked over to her. "Do we...do we know each other?"

"No." Her reply, short and curt, was disappointing.

No more so than her way of dismissing him: by turning her back on him and walking away.

Maybe it was for the best. As attractive as she was, the last thing he needed was to get involved with an AA parent...

But she's not. She told me that...

But when?

Where have I seen her?

He turned around when he heard Miranda's laugh. She was staring straight at him. Apparently, she'd seen it all.

God, I hate her.

CHAPTER 8

"Audrey! I wasn't expecting to see you here today!" Harris rose from the couch in his district office in order to give her a hug, then beckoned Audrey to sit beside him. Some of his upcoming position pages were spread out on the coffee table in front of him.

"I just came in to get a couple of things from my desk." Audrey hesitated, then added, "And to tell you that I'll be taking a leave of absence from work."

"Getting over a parent's death is…it's a big thing. Take as much time as you need—a month, two if necessary."

"It may be longer than just a couple of months." Audrey walked over and sat down beside him. "Lavinia was the only parent I knew. But I also have a father some-where—at least, I hope he's still alive. Lavinia never revealed his name, not even at the end. I…I think it's important to find out." Misty-eyed, she sniffled, "I guess I'm not ready to be an orphan."

Before her eyes, Harris seemed to collapse.

Had he not already been seated he might have fallen to

the floor. He covered his face with his hands as if he was too ashamed for her to see his tears.

His deep heaving sobs startled Audrey. "Harris, I'm so sorry! It was cruel of me to spring this on you this way. You were Lavinia's closest, dearest friend! Of course, your grief is just as deep as mine."

Harris raised his head. Because they were only inches apart, she could hear him as he whispered, "Audrey, *I* am your father."

Harris.

Of course.

Other than Lavinia, he'd been the one constant presence in Audrey's life: for her birthdays and graduations, at many of Lavinia's summer open houses and Thanksgiving gatherings, even on most Christmas Eves.

"But…then, why didn't you and Lavinia marry?"

"We always loved each other. But I saw my destiny as serving in public office—something that frustrated your mother to no end." He sighed. "The thought of being merely a politician's wife—to smile sweetly, say nothing, and keep to the background—was anathema to her. She wanted to change the world her way—one child at a time. I understood that, and I respected it. But that didn't lessen my love for her—or for you."

"Still, you never acknowledged me," Audrey pointed out.

"I would have! Please believe me when I say that! But by the time Lavinia told me she was pregnant, I'd already married Tracy—on the rebound, I guess." He shrugged. "You were a dream come true for Lavinia. Still, she insisted she didn't want her pregnancy to end my dream, my goals. She knew if our secret ever got out, I'd be pilloried by my opponents and by the press. I'd be 'the

Congressman with the love child.' It wasn't something she wanted for any of us. Certainly not Tracy. My wife could never have a child. Lavinia insisted she was never going to tell and urged me to keep silent about it as well."

Just like I'm urging Egan to keep quiet about the twins, Audrey realized.

She remembered the night, those many years ago, when Egan made his triumphant return to Berkeley to read excerpts from his bestselling novel. How he and she had finally talked through all their misunderstandings and missed opportunities. How he'd declared, *I misread so many signals.*

It was the same night he'd gotten her pregnant.

How many misunderstandings, how many missed opportunities, had Lavinia and Harris shared? Did they regret that their paths had diverged at such a significant milestone—the birth of their child?

Despite this, my mother and father did what they felt was right at the time.

And so did I.

Harris' pain is Egan's too.

"Tracy…" Audrey murmured. "Does she know?"

"Tracy has always suspected. But she's never asked. I don't think she wanted to know the truth. She's always embraced the perks of the office." He grimaced at the thought.

Harris' wife had always been kind to Audrey, if distant. Now she knew why.

"I should have played a much bigger part in your life. For that, I ask for your forgiveness." Weighted with regret, Harris' head fell to his chest. "I'll accept anything you want to do about it. In fact, Lavinia and I had one set rule: once you knew about this, the decision would be yours. If retiring from Congress will rectify this, I'll do it."

"Lavinia wouldn't have wanted that, and neither do I." Audrey placed her hand on his cheek. "Knowing you're my father gives me one more reason to love you, Harris."

Hope filled Harris' eyes. "If Lavinia's death proved one thing, it's that we are all pawns of Fate. I want to spend more time with you, Audrey, and your family. I hope you'll allow me to make up for some of the time we've lost."

"Being in public office doesn't mean we won't be in your life. And besides, look at all the good you've accomplished while in office!"

"Thank you for that." He rose, nudging her to do so too. "You've been a part of my life's work for a long time— twenty years now. Please take as much time off to grieve as you need. But I do hope you eventually come back here."

"I will," she promised.

The soft buzz of Harris' cell phone alerted him to a text. He stared down at the caller ID. He frowned, but it was important enough for him to read the message. "Seamus has called for an emergency meeting of AA's trustee board for tomorrow."

"I'm not surprised." Audrey shrugged.

Little by little, the safe, sweet haven that had been her mother's world was turning to ashes.

She hugged Harris before taking her leave.

Invariably, Egan's seventh period students ebbed into his classroom like choppy waves: slowly and singly at first, but when the warning chime rang out, swells of students came in closer together, rolling in several at a time, laughing and gossiping.

Since learning his real role in the twins' lives, Egan's heart swelled at even a glimpse of Charly or Chuck on AA's campus. Usually, Charly's entourage included her closest friends: Sienna Belluci, Manya Patel, and Zina Sisley-Calder. As for Chuck, if he wasn't surrounded by his basketball or baseball teammates, he was locked arm-in-arm with his girlfriend, Fawn McCoppin.

Before, Chuck and Fawn's closeness had been a mere annoyance. Egan knew Fawn was using Chuck as a pawn in one of her mind games, but to what end? Egan wondered when her motive would be revealed.

Knowing that she was one of Miranda's concierge clients didn't help his opinion of her.

And now, thanks to Daniel, Chuck was also ensnared in Miranda's web of corruption.

It would not be easy for Egan to honor his promise to Audrey—that he keep her secret from his children. To do so, he'd have to treat Chuck and Charly like any other student: resist the urge to stare at them in wonder, or to talk to them exclusively. He'd have to tamp down the urge to question them about their childhood, their hopes, dreams, and fears.

He'd have to force himself to look away when they were upset about something, despite the paternal urge to take charge of their young, naïve lives.

I must do this because I promised Audrey.

Egan had every intention of keeping this vow.

But then, when Chuck walked up to him after class and proclaimed, "Miranda said that you can tutor Fawn and me together, since we're both in her concierge program and your free period and our lunch time coincide."

Egan cocked a brow. "Miranda said that, did she?"

Fawn nodded. "Yep. She said you'd make it easy-peasy too."

Egan had been lucky enough to avoid Miranda since their tryst. But the emergency trustee board meeting scheduled for that evening meant he'd be face-to-face with her sooner than he'd hoped.

Coolly, he muttered, "Well, she's wrong. I'm not getting paid to coddle you. I'm helping you pass your most important test this year. I expect you to give it your all."

Chuck saluted, adding, "Hey, no worries! I'm bringing my A game."

On the other hand, Fawn frowned. Confusion was etched in her face.

Had Seamus given her a heads-up about the cheating?

If so, it would be a shame. Miranda hadn't said so, but her scheme had to include more than cheating on SATs to guarantee admission to a top pick university.

No kid should feel that their parent doesn't believe in them, Egan thought.

Because Debate Team practice ran late, Egan made it into the trustee board room just in time to hear Bliss exclaim, "Seamus, explain to me why you think it's so important to have a board meeting tonight, despite there not being a full roster of board members to vote on anything!" Her voice seemed to be cracking under the weight of the past week's events.

Egan looked around the room. Tallulah and Daniel were missing, but Warner was there, as were Jess and Harris.

All heads were turned to Seamus and Bliss.

Miranda was there too. When she nodded to him, he ignored her.

"Bylaws state that any trustee can call a meeting in twenty-four hours if seconded by another." He nodded at Jess, who smiled. "Look, I can't help it that your friends are shirking their duty!"

"My friends are grieving," Bliss retorted. "I'm sure Daniel is doing what he can to hold Audrey together—"

Hearing that made Egan's heart ache.

"—and Tallulah is at the hospital with her mother."

Egan stuttered, "What…what happened?"

"Maggie…she's had a relapse."

"By that, do you mean 'overdose?'" Seamus sneered.

"You…*you monster*!" But Bliss' stutter was proof he'd guessed right. "Her dearest friend died suddenly—or have you forgotten that?"

"Tallulah isn't here to hold your hand. Big deal!" Seamus argued. "Since we last met, Ashbury Academy is in a shambles! One board member was murdered in cold blood and the school's headmistress is dead and buried!" Seamus leaned across the table as if his looming hulk could cower her. "We also have to choose Lavinia's replacement."

"Sorry I'm late." Daniel stood in the doorway. There were dark shadows under his eyes. Where he'd always attended in a suit and tie, today he was in jeans, a sweater, and sneakers.

Bliss was right, Egan thought. He'd stayed home to comfort Audrey.

Daniel took a quick glance around the room. "Since we now have a quorum, I'd like to call the meeting to order."

Seamus wasted no time in making his case: "We need to find Lavinia's replacement as soon as possible."

"I think we're all in agreement on that," Daniel murmured. "I move that we hire a couple of headhunters to line up some appropriate candidates. At the same time, we'll form a search committee made up of staff, parents, and board members. The committee will vet at least three possible candidates before the board interviews them and takes a final vote."

Seamus snorted. "To hell we will! We have great talent on staff, so why not utilize it?"

Bliss frowned. "You mean, hire internally?"

He nodded. "Sure, why not? It'll save a lot of time—something that's in short supply these days."

"Our most important function is the wellbeing of AA's students," Bliss snapped. "The Head of School is AA's guardian, leader, and biggest draw for attracting new families. If you don't feel you have the time for a national search, perhaps you shouldn't be on the board to begin with."

"If you believe so strongly in Lavinia's so-called 'mission,' you should trust in the team she's put together," Seamus retorted. "Our graduates are proof of that. Would you not agree?"

Bliss merely shrugged. She couldn't argue the point.

Seamus grinned smugly. "That's why I recommend we make Miranda the new Head of School."

Egan almost fell out of his chair.

No fucking way!

Whereas Jess and Warner's heads bobbed in agreement, Bliss and Harris' faces mirrored Egan's concern.

Egan couldn't read Daniel's reaction because his head was down as he scribbled notes on the pad in front of him.

As for Miranda, she stared demurely at her clasped hands. Still, her slight grin was the telltale sign that she was in on Seamus' scheme.

And probably Warner and Jess too, Egan deduced.

Seamus is giving her coverage so that she can get away with her college admissions shenanigans, he realized. I won't—I *can't*—let them.

"Big mistake!" Egan exclaimed. "She's too new. And she works primarily with seniors and juniors, so half the kids don't even know her!"

"Their parents do, either by her interaction with them directly, or by reputation—and they think she hung the moon. Her track record speaks for itself," Seamus countered. "So if, as Ms. Thackeray so eloquently put it, the damn kids come first, why screw up the rest of their school year searching for some clone of Lavinia when what we all want is right here already?"

Egan snorted. "By 'what we all want,' you mean someone you feel will guarantee your child is accepted into a prestigious university?"

"Of course, you fool!" Seamus bellowed. "Why do you think we're all here?"

Bliss glared back. "Not necessarily. Most of us are here because we love the school for achieving what Lavinia set out to do with it: teaching students to think for themselves, follow their dreams, and attain their goals—with or without attending a prestigious university."

Silence thickened the tension in the room.

Daniel turned to Miranda. "I assume you've already discussed your interest with Seamus"—his eyes scanned Warner and Jess—"and others as well."

"They approached me, yes," she acknowledged. "I told them how much this school means to me. It molded me into the person I am! But to be honest, giving up my client base will mean a pay cut for me, so there is that to consider." Miranda's sigh made Egan flinch. "As long as I can honor my commitment to my private clients, I'll accept the position of Interim Head of School while a national search is conducted."

No shit.

"I assume Miranda will also feel free to put her name in the hat for the permanent position?" Seamus barked.

Daniel shrugged. "Of course she will."

"Then yes, Daniel. In fact, *I'd be honored* to be Interim Head of School."

Egan marveled at how easily Miranda could make her eyes mist up.

Miranda added, "After all, Lavinia's purpose in hiring me in the first place was to groom me as her successor."

Like Egan, Bliss gawked openly at this revelation.

Daniel frowned. "Funny, she never mentioned that to me. Or to Audrey for that matter."

"*Really?*" Miranda shook her head in disbelief. "Are you sure Audrey has been completely honest with you?"

Daniel stared back.

Finally, shaking his head, he muttered, "Let's put it to vote—specifically, that we offer Miranda the position of *Interim* Head of School while we conduct a national search for Lavinia's permanent replacement."

Reluctantly, Seamus raised his hand. "I second the motion," he huffed.

Daniel shook his head in disgust. "All in favor?"

As anticipated, Warner's and Jess' hands went up too.

"Opposed?" Daniel asked.

Harris and Bliss raised their hands.

Miranda's gaze went to Egan.

When he also raised his hand, her crocodile tears seemed to vanish in the heat of her glare.

Bliss murmured, "Daniel, how do you vote?"

Daniel shrugged. "I support the motion for Miranda to step in as Interim Head of School."

Egan leaned back, aghast.

So, Daniel has paid Miranda to cheat on Chuck's behalf.

It was the only rational reason for Daniel to vote for Miranda to take his beloved mother-in-law's place, even on a temporary basis.

Audrey doesn't know.

She can't.

She would never allow him to do that to her son…

Our son.

Egan tamped down his anger.

It wasn't easy, not with Seamus smugly crowing: "Congratulations, Miranda. Now, I guess we should talk about replacements for the open positions on the trustee board…"

I can do it now, before this whole thing comes down around me, Miranda realized.

I can ruin Egan and Audrey.

Daniel had hesitated when he handed her the gavel. That didn't bother her. She knew she'd be getting her revenge on him and his wife when Egan substituted Chuck's SAT test.

I'll be getting the SAT answer key tomorrow. Afterward, I'll order Egan to meet me at my place, perhaps on Saturday night.

He won't dare say no—

Not now that I control every source of his income.

If Miranda ever got angry enough with Egan, she might even tell him she was Mandy. She'd crow about the pleasure it gave her to have his publisher pull his book from the shelves. She enjoyed that even more than the settlement money.

Well, almost.

While relishing this thought, she'd tuned out the bickering around her, which had begun when Seamus and Egan volleyed suggestions for the staff member who would replace her. It was finally decided that Cornell would do. Seamus saw him as innocuous and controllable. Miranda could tell that Egan thought the same.

She relished the opportunity to prove him wrong.

By now the bickering was *sooo* damn loud that it was distracting from her jubilation. Apparently, Seamus was going nose-to-nose with Bliss as to who should take over as the new parent board member candidate.

"My wife, Gretchen, is perfect!" Seamus insisted. "And besides, she has been the best fundraising chairperson this school has ever had."

"I want to nominate Gemma Sisley," Bliss insisted. "We should do it out of respect for the loss of her husband, who served the board admirably."

Egan was surprised she could state that with a straight face.

"I disagree," Seamus countered. "If anything, she's probably all torn up about it—too much so to consider being on the board—"

Miranda interjected, "I'd like to propose a compromise candidate."

The room went silent.

I could get used to this.

Too bad I can't—unless it's in some Federal prison yard.

She closed her eyes to erase that horrifying vision from her mind. "I think Nira Patel would make a wonderful trustee."

Bliss shrugged her approval. Seamus did the same.

"All in favor?" Miranda asked.

The vote was unanimous.

Only Egan caught the wink between Seamus and Miranda.

"$\mathcal{N}$ormal," Audrey insisted to Daniel. "The sooner we get back into our routines, the better."

It was Friday—only two days since Lavinia's funeral. Still, Audrey had insisted that the children go back to school.

And that Daniel go back to work.

His nod was reluctant at best. "I know you're right. It's just that..." Daniel looked away. "Lavinia's death was so sudden, and it happened only a week ago. I don't feel we've had a chance to process it."

"By 'we,' you mean me, specifically." Audrey glanced away. She'd yet to tell him that Lavinia had told her about the cancer on the very first day of the school year.

She certainly wasn't going to do so now. What would it matter anyway?

"Okay, we'll honor your wishes," Daniel conceded. "But 'normal' should mean doing something fun as well. Why don't we have dinner out as a family? Say, Little Star Pizza. The one on Divisadero."

He knew it was her favorite.

Audrey shrugged. "Sounds good to me." She didn't mean it. She hadn't had an appetite in over a week. Between Lavinia's death and her admission to Egan about the twins, she'd been too upset to even think about eating. "I'll pick up Noah after basketball practice. Then we'll swing by AA and pick up the twins. See you there."

Daniel kissed her. "Stay in bed as long as you like. I'll get the kids to school."

"I will. But…at some point, I have to go over to Lavinia's house and…and start clearing it out."

She hated the thought of putting the house on the market. She was born and raised there.

"Not today," he insisted. "Do it tomorrow. The kids and I will meet you there after our bike ride."

Audrey nodded. She was fine with that. She'd need the day to force herself out of her fear that life as she knew it was at an end.

By the time Audrey and Noah got to AA, it was already past six o'clock.

They found parking one block from the school. Originally, Audrey thought they might wait for the twins in the car, but Noah nixed that by complaining of the cold.

"Look! Even my words are freezing," he insisted, pointing to his chilled breath. "Can't we go in? *Please?*"

Reluctantly, she got out of the car and followed him into the school.

Because it was late on Friday, the school was practically empty. The lobby seemed to have been decorated. Colorful cards filled its large Palladian windows.

For Thanksgiving perhaps? It was only a week away…

When she got close enough to read them, she realized the students had written down fond memories of Lavinia.

"Mom—they're talking about Lavinia!" Noah pointed up to the intercom.

Audrey realized they were listening to students relaying their memories about her mother.

This tribute must have been going on all week, she realized.

As she wiped away a tear, she made a mental note to ask Clare for copies of everything—the notes, the photos, and the audio tribute.

Egan was right when he said Lavinia changed the world of everyone she touched, Audrey realized. She lives on through all of us.

Had the Debate Team practice been held in Egan's classroom, he would never have run into Audrey.

As it turned out, he'd secured the smaller of AA's two auditoriums so that the team could practice on a stage and at a podium.

After seven matches, the team was undefeated. As opposed to playing favorites with the twins, he found himself being even harder on them than their teammates.

Well, harder on Chuck, anyway. Unlike Charly, who always came prepared, Chuck's habit was to review the research for his topic at the last minute. He also played to the audience as opposed to sticking to his talking points.

"You'll be judged by how clearly you make your case. Winking to some hottie in the front row isn't going to win over the judges," Egan warned him.

"Unless she happens to *be* a judge," Quest countered.

His interruption earned him Egan's glare. "Don't encourage him," Egan snapped. Turning to Chuck, he continued: "Look, I know you don't want to let your team down. So do us a favor: *pull your weight.*"

"Wow! That's harsh, Egan," Fawn exclaimed. But by the way she winked at him, she must have appreciated being called a hottie.

"No harsher than his teammates will be if he blows AA's chances to win the regional tournament," Egan retorted.

Chuck nodded stoically. "Okay, yeah, I get it! I'll treat it like a test instead of like…fun."

Egan rolled his eyes. "That's the spirit."

The team's titters at Chuck's exclamation roiled into belly laughs at Egan's sarcasm.

Shaking his head, Egan glanced at the auditorium's clock. "What say we call it a night? But please be ready again on Monday. Remember, it'll be the last practice before our next match. Have a great weekend, everybody."

As the others filed out, Egan fell into line behind Chuck and Fawn. Tapping Chuck's shoulder, he asked, "May I have a word in private?"

Surprised, Chuck nodded.

Fawn pouted but took the hint and stalked up the aisle without him.

Egan waited until she was out of hearing range to say, "I think you have the potential to be anything in this world you want. But if you keep selling yourself short by getting lazy—you'll blow it, plain and simple."

Chuck shrugged. "You sound like my dad."

Egan blinked away his compulsion to blurt out, *that's because I am your father.*

Instead, he muttered, "All that proves is that we both believe in you."

Mollified, Chuck murmured, "Gee, thanks, Egan. I...I appreciate that."

"Good, because there's something I wish to propose. Although Tuesday is a half day because of the Thanksgiving break, I'd like you to hang around an extra hour or so to do some SAT drills. Are you up for that?"

"Yeah sure, I guess." Chuck's eyes followed Fawn out the door. "Are you asking Fawn too?"

"I was under the impression that the McCoppins head down to Laguna Beach every Thanksgiving." He'd heard Seamus discussing that with Warner. "It's not like you two are joined at the hip or anything, is it?"

"No...of course not!" Chuck shrugged. "I doubt she would have wanted to waste the afternoon doing it anyway. She seems to think she has it in the bag."

I'll bet she does.

Egan wanted to ask Chuck to elaborate but he noticed Noah was walking toward them.

Audrey and Charly were heading down the aisle as well.

Audrey's face was placid, but shadows still darkened her eyes. Other than that, she was as beautiful as always.

Egan gave her a slight wave. She nodded back.

When Noah reached Chuck's side, he high-fived his older brother.

"Hey, are you ready to go?" Noah asked. "We're meeting Dad at Little Star."

A pang of jealousy pricked at Egan.

"Sure." Chuck turned to his teacher. "We're done here, right?"

"Yep." Egan forced a smile onto his face. "Enjoy your dinner."

But before he could walk away, Charly tapped him on the arm. "Egan, I was just telling Mom that you came up with the idea for the students remembering Lavinia with the pictures and audio tribute."

Audrey smiled up at him. "I want to thank you for that. I'm touched that you suggested it."

Egan deflected her thanks with a shrug. "I thought it would be a good way for the students to process their grief. I'm glad the other teachers agreed with me."

Chuck reached for the car keys dangling from his mother's hand. "I'll pull the car around, if you want."

Charly snatched the keys from him. "Um—*NO*. It's my turn to drive! Remember?"

Chuck held them up high so that she couldn't reach them.

Charly tickled him so that he'd drop his hand. Instead, he ran up the aisle with them.

She took off after him.

Noah was on her heels—

Leaving Audrey alone with Egan.

She looks so…sad.

"How are you holding up?" he asked.

"I'll be better after…after the holidays, I guess." She sighed. "I'll wait to tackle Lavinia's house afterward."

"You're selling it?"

"We have to." Audrey's eyes grew damp. "I grew up in that house. But it was her wish. And it will go a long way in establishing the endowment. It's worth close to two million dollars." Suddenly, her tears were falling fast and furiously. "The kids are upset. They'd rather I didn't."

"Oh, Audrey, I'm so, so sorry!" Egan put his arms around her. "Cleaning out a parent's home...it's not easy. Every item in it comes with some memory."

He knew this from experience. When his father died, his mother refused to get rid of any of her husband's belongings.

When she was moved into the care facility, the sale of the house was necessary to keep her there. Egan had to tackle the task of cleaning out the home himself.

The worst part was his parents' closets. Their scents lived on in his father's business suits and in his mother's cocktail dresses, bringing to life his memories of them as younger, vital people.

It struck Egan that when his time came, there would be no one to do the same for him.

Without thinking, Egan stroked Audrey's hair.

At first, she sighed at the tender act.

But too soon, she stepped away.

It was for the best, Egan reasoned. Not with what I need to mention next. "Listen, Audrey—we have to talk."

Warily, Audrey murmured, "What about?"

"I can't say in front of the children," he insisted.

"Egan please! You're not going to insist again that I tell them...and... Daniel—"

"This has nothing to do with that," he promised, he motioned for her to walk with him. "Did Daniel mention what went on during the trustee meeting last night?"

Perplexed, Audrey shook her head. "I was worn out and went to bed early. And this morning, with getting the kids ready for school and all..." She shrugged. "Daniel didn't mention it, and I forgot to ask."

"Lavinia's successor was named."

Audrey shook her head in disbelief. "But...a search would need to be conducted first."

"Half the board would agree with you—at least, the half that voted against it and lost."

Obviously Daniel wants to keep it from her. But she has every right to know. Just tell her.

Egan paused, wondering if he should just come out and tell her whom. Finally, he added: "Seamus and his contingent pushed for Miranda."

Audrey frowned. "Miranda D'Arcy—*the college admissions counselor*? Why her?"

He shrugged. "They feel she is best positioned to get their children into the colleges of their choice. And"—Egan took a deep breath—"they may be right, but for all the wrong reasons."

"What do you mean?"

"Before I answer that, let me ask you a question. Did Lavinia ever indicate to you that she was grooming Miranda as her successor?"

Audrey shook her head. "Not in the least! I mean, she thought Miranda was a good hire. And as you know, at the time, Lavinia already knew she was sick. But she would never have just handed over the reins to someone who didn't have the approval of the school community, let alone someone who didn't fit her philosophy for the school."

Egan snorted. "Trust me. She doesn't. Which was why I was just as dumbfounded as Bliss and Harris when Daniel voted to go along with Seamus' cockamamie plan—as Interim Head, anyway."

"*Daniel* voted for her too?" Audrey's shock at this revelation revealed itself with a shudder. Noting his concern, she murmured, "Egan, what are you trying to say?"

Tell her. Everything.

He would have, too, if a car horn hadn't blared just then.

They looked up to find that Chuck was parked in front of the school.

"Ask Daniel how much he paid for Chuck to be in Miranda's concierge program, okay?"

"But…her counseling services are supposed to be gratis to AA's students. It's why she was hired in the first place."

"I said ask him what he paid for her concierge program —which is altogether different, trust me." He moved in close to make his point. "Please Audrey, just ask."

Audrey frowned. "Okay, I will." Waving at her children, Audrey ran out the door.

"Isn't that nice! You've had a few precious moments alone with your heartthrob!"

Startled by Miranda's voice, Egan took a step backward before turning to face her.

She almost laughed at the pained look on his face.

"No need to be jealous," he retorted. "We were discussing Chuck's progress."

"If that's what you call those loving strokes to her hair, I'm surprised every mother in the school isn't lining up at your door to get an update." She laughed. "As for Chuck, don't you mean 'lack thereof?' Not that it will show up on his SAT score." She moved closer in order to stroke his cheek. "Speaking of which, I'll have the test's answer key for you later tonight, along with the final list of my clients.

Why don't you drop by my place and pick it up—say, eight o'clock?"

Egan took a step back. "We've already had this discussion. My duties as your concierge program's SAT coach and proctor don't come with fringe benefits. Just hand it off to me on Monday, here at school."

Miranda clicked her tongue in mock shock. "As of last night's vote, I'm your boss here at AA too. Remember? And, as such, you're at my beck and call—*including tonight.*" Her palm brushed against his bulge. "And don't think I wasn't hurt when you voted against me. I should fire you over it."

"Is that a threat?"

"You bet it is," Miranda declared. "Quit playing games, Egan. We both know you're strapped for cash. When I offered you the position of proctor, I offered you a lifeline. The money is plentiful and easy. *You don't want to fuck this up.*" Her hand cupped the bulge in his jeans.

Suddenly Egan's open palm came toward her face—

Stopping a mere inch from her cheek.

Instinctively, Miranda reeled back, as much from fear as shock.

Egan lowered his arm, but he was still seething with anger. "Don't ever touch me like that again," he growled. "Fire me, if you want. But if you do, I'll walk from both jobs."

He waited until she nodded.

"Just leave the information in my staff mailbox," he said, slamming the front door behind him.

That son of a bitch.

And all because he's still in love with her.

By the time Miranda reached Lavinia's office—*her* office—her heart had quit pounding in her chest. Still seething with anger, she took the only photo on the credenza—one of Lavinia in the loving arms of the Thorpe-McKittridge clan—and hurled it to the floor.

Shards flew everywhere as the frame's glass crashed into pieces. As she reached to pick up the mess, one pierced her palm.

Miranda cursed "BLOODY HELL—" at the top of her lungs.

It's all Egan's fault.

His—and Audrey's.

Time for payback.

She walked into Clare's office and over to the massive file credenza behind her desk. Finding the drawer labeled DONATIONS, she pulled out the file folder earmarked:

TEACHER CHAIR - ENDOWMENT

It went into the shredder.

She had several offshore bank accounts. One was an emergency account that contained a mere three hundred thousand dollars.

From that account, she transferred $250,000 to The Best Face Forward Club.

It was earmarked

Donation - McKittridgge D. (Chuck)

The last fifty thousand dollars was transferred from the personal account to another she had registered to one of her fake names: Pucci Tedeschi. That way, there would be no trace of where the so-called donation had come from.

However, when the FBI discovered it, she'd reluctantly admit it was from Daniel.

On Monday, when the announcement that she'd been selected as the new Interim Head of School would be made public, everything and everyone would fall in line.

Including Egan.

Miranda would have access to the school's bank accounts. She'd shuffle funds into new ones set up and controlled by her.

Seamus would only be given some of the account information.

The FBI would be given a different story.

She didn't know how—*yet*—but hopefully, when the money trail went cold, she'd be long gone—

Along with the missing funds.

Audrey and Daniel would have a heck of a time explaining away the contribution. And by the time they did, Daniel may have lost his law firm partnership, perhaps even his license to practice law.

And when it came out that Egan had substituted Chuck's test—at the behest of Daniel, in fact—Mr. McKittridge and Ms. Thorpe would have reason to hate each other.

Their family would live in disgrace.

If I have to go down, they're going down with me.

"Miranda's assessment and tutoring for Chuck—is that something we're paying for?" Audrey waited until they were home from dinner and were reading in bed before doing as she'd promised Egan.

Daniel put down the brief he'd been studying. "Nope. Why do you ask?"

"During the first PTA meeting, Miranda mentioned some sort of 'concierge counseling program' she has for her private clients. I was wondering if she'd talked you into it."

Daniel shook his head. "All she offered was what we wanted: that Chuck be given extra attention on his SAT drills. But if her special program could help Chuck buckle down before he takes the test, should we consider it?"

"I don't think there's time to schedule it. The final SAT test takes place in two weeks. And besides, Chuck mentioned in the car that his first coaching session with Egan is on Tuesday. Why don't we see how that goes first and then panic?"

Daniel guffawed. "I guess you're right. By then, it would be too late for Miranda to pull off a miracle anyway —although Seamus and Jess seem to think she could under any circumstances. Warner too."

"No wonder she has the trustee board wrapped around her little finger," Audrey muttered.

"What do you mean by that?" Daniel asked.

"Egan mentioned that the trustee board voted her as the interim replacement for Lavinia until a nationwide search can take place."

Daniel shrugged. "It did indeed."

She turned to him. "Did you vote for her too?"

Daniel grimaced. "What, Egan didn't tell you?"

"No, but I didn't ask either." She frowned. "I thought the answer would be obvious."

"I guess it isn't, since, yes, I did vote for her."

"But why? If Harris and Tallulah and Bliss thought a search would be a better solution–"

"You forgot to include Egan," Daniel snapped back.

Audrey felt her cheeks warming up.

"By the way, Tallulah wasn't there," Daniel continued. "Maggie is in rehab. She took Lavinia's death pretty hard."

"Oh! I didn't know." Audrey's shoulders slumped. "Look, Daniel, I guess the point I'm trying to make is that obviously, my friends felt uncomfortable with just handing over the reins of the school to someone who is still learning the AA community."

"Anyone brought in from a nationwide search will be in the same position," he pointed out. "In that regard, Miranda has a head start—and at least the confidence of half the board." Daniel tossed the brief to the floor. "I suppose this is your way of telling me that your 'proxy' made the wrong choice."

"You aren't my proxy," Audrey protested.

Yes, you were. THAT WAS THE DEAL.

"You're right. I'm not," Daniel retorted. "I took the position under my own free will—and with your blessing, I might add. So it would be nice if you—and Egan—didn't second-guess me."

"This has nothing to do with Egan!" Audrey retorted hotly. "It's just that…well, I've been skeptical of Seamus' motives since he enrolled Fawn. You know that. And for that matter, there's something about Miranda that's a bit off-putting as well. And I'm not the only one who's noticed."

"If you mean Bliss and Tallulah—"

"And Harris," Audrey added.

"Okay, yes, and Harris—then I guess I screwed up. But

I felt that, at the very least, Miranda—as a stop-gap measure—was the most viable and least traumatic option."

"But that's just it! Seamus ultimately wants her as Lavinia's permanent replacement—and *you* were okay with that!" Audrey's tears flowed now. "As if that…that woman could ever replace Lavinia!"

"No one can replace Lavinia! Everyone—even Seamus—knows that!" Daniel reached for Audrey's hand. "Lavinia's death was so sudden. You—and I, and the kids—are still processing it!" He pulled her close. "I didn't want you to have to worry about the school too. I told Seamus and his group Miranda was only a temporary fix."

Audrey nodded. "I appreciate that. Truly I do. But even on an interim basis, I hope it was the right decision."

"Believe me, I do too," Daniel murmured.

CHAPTER 10

On Monday morning, waiting in Egan's school mailbox designated for Egan was a large manila envelope.

It contained the SAT answer sheet, along with the final names of the students whose tests were to be substituted:

Chuck McKittridge
Buck Crawford
Hugo Smallwood
Zina Sisley-Calder
Fawn McCoppin
Quest Wishart-Jammerhead
Manya Patel

On Tuesday, to Egan's great relief, after the school let out at noon for the Thanksgiving break, Chuck showed up on time for his SAT coaching session.

He would have been disappointed if Chuck had let him down.

Granted, on Chuck's first drill, a language test, he barely made an acceptable score. However, he did a lot better on the math test.

The essay test was passable too.

After the initial drills, Egan declared, "Okay, let's start with some simple tips for the language portion."

Chuck nodded.

"First off, use the process of elimination. Since only one answer can be right, immediately eliminate the three that are the weakest."

"Gotcha," Chuck murmured.

"Also, skim first. You do this by starting with the first and last paragraphs and then reading the first and last sentences in each paragraph. Then see if you can answer the main question first. The other questions will reference smaller details, so their keywords will be reflected in what you've just read."

"Okay."

"And all answers will be backed up by evidence presented in one of the paragraphs. If not, it's wrong."

Chuck nodded slowly. "Can I try one?"

Egan handed him another language test question. "Go at it."

This time, he answered all but one of the questions correctly. But on the next three drill sheets, all were correct.

Hearing this, Chuck leaped out of his seat, triumphant.

"Calm down, cowboy. We still have a long way to go," Egan warned. "Okay, now let's address your math score. Granted, from your math grades these past couple of years, you have a good comprehension of geometric and algebraic principles. The questions you missed were incorrectly calculated because you went for the wrong value. I'd suggest re-visiting as many formulas as possible. You can do that now. Then you can try your hand at a few practice questions."

"On it."

They took the next half hour reviewing a list of formulas. Then Chuck tackled a few more problems.

After handing them back to Egan to grade, he waited anxiously for the results.

Finally, Egan declared, "Correct, on all of them."

"*YESSSS!*" Chuck exclaimed proudly.

The next hour was spent going over the weaknesses in his essay.

"You have no issues with grammar or spelling. Your weakness is making your case succinctly, then backing it up with evidence."

Chuck snickered. "Just like on Debate Team."

"Ironically, yes." Egan grinned. "Now, knowing this, use the rules I've tried to pound into you during debate practice: come up with three facts or examples. Save the strongest for last. Got it?"

"Yep." Chuck cracked his knuckles. "Let's do this thing."

After four test questions, Egan declared that Chuck had nailed it. He glanced at the clock. It was almost three-thirty. "Now that you've got the hang of this thing, what say we call it a day?"

Chuck nodded. "It seemed to have gone by pretty quickly. Wow, can you believe we've been here three hours?" He grabbed his backpack and stood up. "Hey, Egan, what do you do for Thanksgiving? I mean, like, is your family back in New York?"

No. My family is right here.

You are my family.

Chuck hesitated, then added somewhat bashfully: "I'd

hate for you to spend it by yourself. I mean...you're welcome to hang out with us."

Thanksgiving with Chuck and Charly—

And Audrey.

"Thanks. That's very kind of you, but... I'm covered," Egan muttered. "I'll be at my mother's house."

Eating something from the Greenbrae Mollie Stone's deli after spending an hour watching her nurse feed her while I remind her who I am.

Chuck nodded. "Oh! Good, then." But he seemed disappointed.

At least, that's what Egan wanted to believe.

He consoled himself with the thought that Chuck was ready for his test; that when his son saw his grade, he'd believe he did well on it because he'd studied hard for it.

The following week, Egan also arranged one-on-one after-school coaching sessions with Miranda's other concierge students.

Hugo and Buck skipped their appointments. Egan realized they were in on their parents' schemes.

For their turns, Zina, Manya, and Quest showed up promptly.

Manya's issues were not with the test subjects, but with her fear of failure.

"I can't let my mother down!" Manya explained. "She has been working so hard to pay for my tuition—even if I'm lucky enough to get accepted to her alma mater, Stanford." Her anxiety was accompanied by tears. "If I don't earn a scholarship—especially to there—she'll be so disappointed."

"You've gotten straight A's every semester you've been at AA. You've taken every Advanced Placement course the school offers. You're brilliant, Manya!" Egan insisted. "If you're freezing when you take the SAT, it's because you're psyching yourself out. Today, we'll go over some tips that should help you focus on the questions, as opposed to your fears. Okay?"

She nodded.

"Afterward, we'll do a few practice tests in each section. I'm not going to time the drills, so take as long as you like."

She took a deep breath. "Okay."

He lied.

So, when he gave her the test scores—the first one was 1408, while the second was 1466—he also let her know she turned them in well under the time usually allotted.

Hearing that, she burst into tears of joy.

Egan was also elated—

Until she anxiously exclaimed, "I wish these had counted."

Egan shrugged. "You can take it as often as you like. In fact, why don't you first take the last one offered with the rest of your class on Saturday? Then you take the test I'll be administering on Sunday. That way, you'll have two chances at a great score. The highest one will be counted."

Her eyes opened wide. "Great idea!"

She hugged him before going out the door.

How he wished Nira had not fallen for Miranda's line.

Like Manya, Zina suffered from test anxiety. But unlike her friend, she also had low math test scores.

"I feel like an idiot," she muttered. "I know this stuff! Really, I do."

"Just remember, process of elimination is an important strategy when taking the SAT. Three answers will always be wrong. You just have to determine the *right* one. By knowing the formulas, you'll figure it out."

As he did with Chuck, he went over math formulas that would be used on the test, then drilled her on them, again and again.

After each drill, her scores inched up.

Every time she squealed with joy.

As with Manya, he suggested that she take the timed test that was to be given to AA's students. "Use it as another drill. It'll give you even more confidence for the untimed test on Sunday."

She nodded, but he could see she wasn't excited about the idea. Her doubts were creeping back.

During the final drill, Zina's phone chirped. Looking at the caller ID, she frowned. "That's my mom."

"It's okay if you take it," Egan assured her.

She hesitated a moment. When she finally took it, she turned her back and murmured, "Hi, Mom... With, um, Charly... In the library. Can I call you when we get out? ...Sure, see you then."

Seeing Egan's bemused stare, Zina blushed. "Mom doesn't know I'm here."

Egan nodded slowly, perplexed. "Why not?"

"With Dad's death and all, Mom's got enough on her plate." Zina shrugged. "Look, I know the type of clients my dad had. And I know he kept a lot of secrets from her. I didn't want to tell her that this was yet another one. He knew Mom wouldn't approve of Miranda's special concierge program."

"If you don't have your mother's permission, I'm sure Miranda wouldn't hold her to your father's commitment."

"I asked. But Miranda told me that I'd be dishonoring Dad's dying wish, that I should take advantage of his generosity." Zina sighed. "I guess she's right."

That money-grubbing bitch.

"He was very proud of you, Zina. You must believe that! As far as this test goes, if you do well, it's just icing on the cake."

She hung her head. "No, Egan, it's more than that." A tear trickled down her face. "He wanted me to get into *Yale.* So... I'll do my best. Miranda says that together, we're going to make it happen—*for him.*"

And that's how Egan discovered how much more he hated Miranda.

"So, um, what do you think? Is it better than the last drill?" Quest winced as if he didn't really want to hear the answer to that.

Egan shrugged. "It's, um... passable."

The truth was Quest was a hardworking student doomed to mediocre grades.

It took Egan almost three hours and nine drills to accept this reality.

From the hopeful look on Quest's face, saying so would crush the poor kid.

I just can't do it, Egan realized.

"We're all set." He hoped he sounded encouraging, but he doubted it.

Jubilant, Quest leaped up. "Awesome! Can't wait to tell my dad. Have a great night, Egan. And thanks."

Instinctively, he grabbed for the guitar that never left his side.

He strummed a few chords before going into a melodic jazz riff that filled the room.

Egan listened, mesmerized.

This kid is terrific.

Egan clapped. "Wow, that's really beautiful, Quest." He hesitated, but he had to ask: "I know your mom has such great respect for your musical skills. And I would think that a working musician with your chops wouldn't necessarily need a four-year college degree to ply your trade. Was it your idea to go on to college?"

Quest paused mid-riff. "Hell no! And trust me, it wasn't Mom's either." His head shook with his frustration. "My dad says I need a good fallback position in case I don't—you know, make it. He wants me to get into USC's music program. He says that at the very least, I'll be able to teach, or maybe take over the business side of things." He stared down at his guitar. "I can't let him down."

Why that son of a bitch Jammerhead! I have half a notion of telling Tallulah—

But Egan knew it wasn't his place.

Besides, he was just as complicit as Jammerhead. He'd taken the money.

With any luck, Tallulah would never find out. His friendship with her was built on the shifting sands of admiration and antipathy.

Should Miranda's scheme ever be revealed, his role in it would certainly tip the scale far beyond the latter—to animosity.

The silence sat between them until, finally, Egan said, "You won't. You'll be fine."

Quest's relief was shown in a sustained guitar lick that followed him out the door.

Why can't parents accept their kids the way they are, Egan wondered.

Right then and there, he vowed to always do just that with Chuck and Charly.

Egan was surprised when Fawn showed up for her allotted time slot.

He was also impressed with her scores on her initial test drills.

"You already test over 1400," he informed her. "And you've turned these in before the allotted time. Your essay was exemplary."

"Are you asking me if I know I'm smarter than my parents give me credit for?" Fawn smirked. "Like, *duh —yeah!*"

"You also have the cheerleading squad and Debate Team going for you." He threw up his hands perplexed. "So, explain to me. Why again do your parents feel you needed to be placed in Miranda's concierge program?"

Fawn's laugh was venomous. "Because they don't believe I can do it on my own—get into Daddy's alma mater, Yale."

"Fawn, do you believe that too?"

"Who cares what I believe? They're paying for Miranda's guarantee." She shrugged. "Even if I get in, I may not go."

"Out of spite?" Egan murmured.

"Yeah. Exactly." Fawn grinned. "Seriously, though, Egan—what do you care? You get paid, either way, right?"

That's when he realized:

She knows.

And she doesn't care.

On Sunday, all seven of Miranda's concierge students showed up for their SAT test session in AA's small auditorium.

Egan told them to take as much time as they needed on each of the three test sections. Should they finish before the others, they were allowed to wait in the school's lobby.

After completing each of the three test sections, Hugo and Buck were the first out the door.

Buck's attempt was half-hearted at best.

Hugo simply wrote:

Go for it!

Egan wasn't surprised at either boy's actions.

Zina, Manya, and Chuck seemed to take his drill advice to heart. They were excited but not anxious. They worked diligently and carefully. And, had the exams been timed, they would have turned in their tests under the wire. He noted that all had at least attempted every question.

Fawn breezed through each section. However, she left a few questions blank in each section. She turned in the last part, the math portion, with a note:

I left the ones I didn't know blank, to make your life easy. —xoxoxo Fawn

Thanks for nothing, Egan fumed silently.

Only Quest seemed to struggle to complete the test.

By the time he finished the final section, the others were long gone. He seemed relieved, albeit far from happy. "Well, at least I did my best," Quest muttered.

Egan realized he'd have his work cut out for him.

It took four hours to finish the job of doctoring the tests.

Hugo and Buck's real tests were useless. Egan's version gave Hugo a score of 1406. Because of Buck's half-hearted attempt, he scored him around 1401.

He tackled Quest's next. Egan was tempted to give the kid a score of 1430 just because he was so nice, if clueless. He decided it was too big a stretch for anyone who knew him to believe, so he nudged it to 1411 instead.

All three of the boys had lousy handwriting. Still, Egan did his best to copy it, but it was a painstaking endeavor.

The essay portion of the tests for Fawn, Manya, and Zina needed no changes, thank goodness.

Fawn only answered the questions she knew were right. But to get her over a score of 1400, Egan needed to fill in about eighteen more questions: eleven in the math portion and seven in the language section. He estimated that her score would be around 1501.

Manya reached a score of 1508 on her own. Egan left it that way.

He massaged Zina's math answers so that she'd come in at 1436.

He left Chuck's test for last.

Only after Chuck left the room had Egan made a decision: he wasn't going to touch Chuck's test or replace it.

He opened it to look at it, but he didn't touch it otherwise.

I'm turning it in just as it was, along with the others, he vowed. Let the chips fall where they may.

What could Miranda do to him anyway? She'd already paid him the cash. She wouldn't dare ask for it back.

So what if she told Daniel about it? No matter what Chuck scored, Daniel would have to live with the result.

Daniel wouldn't sue Egan. It would be admitting fraud.

If he did, Audrey would know. And in Audrey's eyes, Daniel would be a liar and a cheat.

I have a right to make any decision affecting my son.

———

Lionel bent down to look at Riley's monitor. "That's the video feed of the test session?"

Riley nodded. "I watched it in real-time. It's boring as hell. I'm just adding a few notes."

Because the auditorium was already set up with video cameras, Lionel had secured a subpoena. Riley then hacked into it so that they could watch Egan administer the test.

"Yeah, well, the fun starts after the students leave. That's when Egan tosses their tests and substitutes them with ones he's already filled out," SallyAnne reminded him.

There was no glee in her voice, for good reason: she was genuinely disappointed in him.

It was at that point that the last student—Quest Wishart-Jammerhead—walked out.

Egan sat silently for a moment, sighed, and then pulled out one of the student's tests: From a different camera angle, the agents noted that it was the essay portion of Buck Warner's test.

By the time he'd done the same for Hugo, SallyAnne

couldn't stomach watching any longer. She picked up her valise. "It's been a long night. I think I'll head out."

"No worries." Riley waved Lionel away too. "You can both take off. I got this."

SallyAnne guessed Riley was still feeling guilty for almost blowing his cover at Lavinia's memorial service.

She'd felt guilty too. When Egan saw her at Lavinia's memorial service, he'd walked up to her and asked if they knew each other—in front of Miranda, no less.

Thank goodness he hadn't remembered her.

Still, Miranda had no qualms telling Lionel about it.

Had Egan not been drunk the night they'd met, would he have remembered?

For that matter, would he have accepted Miranda's offer to fix her clients' SAT tests?

I'll never really know, SallyAnne realized.

And yet, she desperately wanted to believe he'd have threatened to expose Miranda, but she knew better.

Even if he had regrets, he would have done so since that night, she reasoned. At least that's what Lionel would argue.

And not just because he's jealous of Egan, either.

That thought put a slight smile on her lips.

"What are you grinning about?" Lionel pushed the elevator button.

Since the cage was already there, it opened immediately. He nodded for SallyAnne to enter first.

"Nothing, really," she answered. "It's been a long day and I'm glad it's over. Until the crack of dawn tomorrow, anyway."

"Hey, want to stop for a bite to eat?"

SallyAnne nodded. "My car is in the shop, and I took the bus. Can you give me a lift home?"

"Sure, no problem." Now Lionel was grinning.

Suddenly SallyAnne realized why. She huffed, "Unlike Miranda's fib to Daniel, I'm telling the truth."

"Frankly, I wouldn't be offended if you weren't," he admitted.

They decided to eat on Polk Street, which was the halfway point between their apartments.

Because it was a Sunday and already after eight, they easily scored a table at Fiorella. They ordered a pizza, a salad, and a glass of wine each.

After a second glass of wine, Lionel found the nerve to come out and ask: "You like him, don't you?"

SallyAnne snickered. "Who...*Riley?*"

Lionel shook his head. "Egan."

SallyAnne took a deep breath. "Let's just say I'm disappointed in him. I guess...my idol has clay feet."

Lionel stifled a grin. "That's truly...well, *biblical.*"

"You're laughing at me," SallyAnne muttered.

"No, not at all. But I am worried about you."

She frowned. "What does that mean?"

"It's just that..." Lionel realized right then that he should have chosen his words with greater care. "We're in this for the long haul—when the acceptances come in and the parents involved lay down money with the schools. That way, we tie everything up with a nice little bow before it goes in front of a jury. I just don't want your... your appreciation of Egan—*as a writer*—to..." He winced, because he didn't know how else to say it: "Well, to cloud your judgment."

I don't want you to fall in love with him.

I want you to fall in love with me.

"How—how dare you!" she sputtered. "After all those little mind games you and Miranda play on each other—"

"'Mind games?'" Lionel couldn't believe his ears. "You have the nerve to accuse me of that? Why, you become a different person around Gable!"

"Is that so? Well then, who am I?" Her question was more than a dare.

"You're a… a lovesick fan! When he came onto you at Lavinia's memorial service, you practically melted!"

"I did no such thing!" Incensed, she added, "And you're a… *A TEASE!*"

As SallyAnne leaped up, her valise fell off the chair beside her, spilling its contents on the floor: file folders, her cell phone, and two spare 9mm magazines for her Sig Sauer.

When they scrambled to retrieve it, Lionel's forehead slammed into the back of her head.

"Dammit!" They exclaimed at the same time.

But when they righted themselves, he saw it for himself: the concern in SallyAnne's eyes.

No, it was pure unadulterated love.

And that's when he kissed her.

At first, she didn't pull away.

But then she did.

Oh shit, he thought. Oh shit.

Shit!

She shoved everything back into her valise and then stumbled out of the restaurant.

He ran after her. "Wait!" he implored.

Now crying, she shook her head. "I'm just a few blocks away! I'll walk!"

"Please, Sally Anne—"

"Lionel, no! I..." She couldn't finish her sentence because she was sobbing so hard.

He wanted to hold her in his arms. But he knew if he did, he'd never want to let her go.

Ever.

So instead, he let her walk away.

SECOND SEMESTER

CHAPTER 11

"Mail!" Noah shouted.

He tossed it on the foyer table with one hand, while grabbing an apple from the bowl placed in the center with another.

The rest of the family was plucking ornaments off the Christmas tree. Usually, it stayed up until Epiphany. The fact that it had browned out more quickly than usual was no surprise, considering that Daniel had insisted on getting the tree the weekend after Thanksgiving in the hope of boosting the family's spirits.

Instead, it had the opposite effect. Although Lavinia wasn't there in person, she was always in their thoughts.

It was the family's tradition that she'd accompany them to get the Christmas trees that would grace their respective homes. The larger of the two trees stood in the Thorpe-McKittridge's picture window. A much smaller tree was placed beside the fireplace in the tiny living room of Lavinia's cottage.

Whereas Lavinia's tree was decorated with the homemade ornaments she'd made with Audrey in their time living together as mother and daughter, each year Lavinia gifted each member of the family a unique ornament—something memorializing an experience she'd shared personally with the recipient.

One year, Charly's ornament was a tiny fishing rod holding a trout, commemorating their grandmother-granddaughter fishing trip when Charly was twelve. At the age of six, Noah's ornament was made of a shell they'd found walking along Ocean Beach. Chuck's decoration for the year he turned eight came from a Giants game that Lavinia had attended with the family. He'd sat beside her and named all the players then regaled her with their stats.

It was Lavinia with whom the children designed and baked a gingerbread house. And her contribution to the Christmas Eve meal was her homemade orange spice cookies, egg nog, and sweet potato soufflé.

But now, with Lavinia gone, the family's attempt at gathering around the piano to sing Christmas carols ended after five minutes. Memories of Lavinia sitting side by side with Charly teaching her *Silver Bells* on the piano and then showing Chuck how to strum along on the guitar while Noah sang along in his angelic contralto left them choking back tears.

Lavinia was everywhere, and they missed her terribly.

So yes, the sooner the tree came down, the better.

"Anything of importance?" Daniel asked.

"This sort of looks official. It's for Chuck." Noah handed his older brother an envelope from College Board, the organization that administered the SAT.

Chuck's eyes grew big.

Everyone froze except for Charly, who ran over to him. "Don't keep us in suspense," she prodded.

Chuck ripped open the envelope's seal and stared down the sheet inside of it.

"Well?" Audrey's voice quivered with anxiety.

"Fifteen-twenty-two," he murmured. He waved the sheet at his mother. *"Wahoo! Fifteen-fuckin' twenty-two!"* His shouts were accompanied by a moonwalk that morphed into a hump dance.

"Watch your language!" Their parents shouted in unison. But soon their screams were just as loud as his.

Rolling her eyes, Charly muttered, "You are *such* a homie wannabe!"

"You're just pissed because I scored higher than you," he retorted.

He was right, and Charly knew it. The fact that she took each test seriously and that she studied long hours to maintain a high grade point average had been the one thing no one could take away from her.

Until now.

Daniel's hug lifted Audrey off the floor. When he set her down again, he high-fived Chuck. "See? I told you! If you focused, you could ace it!"

Suddenly, Chuck's cell phone hummed. He glanced at the screen. "It's Fawn!" he exclaimed. As he walked away toward the foyer, Charly heard him say, "Yeah! I just got mine too!... Fifteen-twenty-two!...What? Fifteen-oh-one? Awesome!"

Fawn tied my score?

Great. Just... great.

I have to get out of here.

No one noticed Charly had left the room.

Charly had just started upstairs to grab her handbag when she heard Chuck's voice behind her. She looked down to see him pacing in the foyer.

I'm silly. The very least I can do is congratulate him.

She was about to start down again when she heard him say: "What do you mean, the whole thing's a sham?"

Charly froze.

"Our parents…they paid to do *what?*….I don't believe you! I mean, Egan drilled with me—for hours! *He worked me hard.*"

Silence.

Then:

"Yeah, well, believe whatever you want." Chuck's voice cracked.

He's angry, Charly thought. What the heck did that girl say to him? What's a sham?

Chuck's footsteps sounded as if he'd turned around and was now coming her way. Charly flattened herself against the wall.

Chuck was scowling. But before he walked back into the living room, he set his mouth into a grin.

She could hear her parents welcoming him back and peppering him with questions.

About his study habits.

About revisiting his college applications to make sure they were current.

About touring a few more campuses.

About his future.

Charly grabbed her coat from her room. When the coast was clear, she tiptoed downstairs and out the front door.

The line at the Kabuki Theater for the latest *Spiderman* movie was so long that Charly, Sienna, Zina, and Manya decided to skip it altogether and hit one of Japantown's karaoke bars instead.

The driver's licenses they showed the bouncer claimed they were over twenty-one. He didn't look closely—a sure sign he probably knew better.

The fake IDs were courtesy of Hugo Warner. He sold them for a hundred dollars apiece.

When Chuck got one, he insisted that Charly do it as well. In fact, he ponied up the cash for it—his way to keep her from tattling about the forgeries.

Although she'd had the ID since last summer, this was the first time she'd used it. In fact, she was so paranoid her parents would somehow come across it that she hid it in a broken seam of her wallet.

Today, it came in handy.

Zina insisted on paying their way into the bar. She also paid for their cocktails—Moscow Mules. She was still on a high from learning she'd scored 1436 on her SAT test.

"Mine was fifteen thirty-six," Manya exclaimed proudly.

"I'll bet your mom is still floating on a cloud!" Sienna had to shout over a college-age couple who were crooning *I've Got You, Babe.*

"Why do you think she let me break curfew tonight?" Manya shouted back.

"Damn! You beat me by *seven points!*" Charly muttered. "And Chuck scored fifteen-twenty-two."

Zina's eyes went wide. "Jeebus! I guess Egan is officially a…oh, I don't know—I guess he's some sort of 'dumb-ass whisperer'!"

Charly scowled. "Chuck isn't dumb! He's just lazy."

Zina thought a moment, then nodded. "Point taken. But I'm not just talking about him. I ran into Buck Warner. He claims he scored over fourteen hundred! Seriously, what are the odds of that? That dude could make a lamppost look like a Rhodes Scholar!" She shook her head in dismay. "He told me Hugo scored over fourteen hundred too."

If Egan had coached me, I might have scored over fifteen-fifty. Maybe even the full sixteen hundred…

Suddenly, Charly wished she'd insisted on being in Miranda's special program too.

Manya's smile, caught in each flicker of the bar's pulsing strobing lights, morphed into a frown.

Charly shook her head. "That can't be! Hugo and Buck walked out halfway through each session of the test—"

Suddenly, she felt her cell phone buzzing in her pocket. She looked down to see who was calling.

Her mother had tried to reach her eight times.

Well, too bad.

For once, she didn't mind that Audrey was worried about her. If being in trouble was the only way to get her parents' attention, then so be it.

"The next round is on me," she exclaimed. She headed to the bar to get four more Mules.

She didn't remember how she got home, or why she'd slept in her clothes, for that matter.

She'd never felt so dizzy in her life either.

At least she'd somehow taken off her shoes. She realized this when she rolled over into something sticky…

And smelly:

Vomit.

"Ugh!" she groaned.

"Ah! You're finally awake."

Charly flinched at the sound of her mother's voice. She opened one eye, then the other. "Do you have to be *so loud?*" The question inched out of her mouth in a hoarse croak.

Audrey sighed. "I just seem loud to you because you're hung over." She held out a glass. "Here, drink this."

Charly stared at the glass, then shook her head. "But it's...*green!*" Just the thought of it touching her lips sent her into dry heaves.

"Trust me. You'll feel much better."

Adamantly, Charly shook her head.

"I'm not leaving until you do."

Finally, Charly groaned, sat up, and did as she was told.

"Good!" Audrey grinned. "Darling, are you really all that upset that Chuck did well on that darn test?"

"No! ... Yes..." Charly stared at her bedspread—not such a smart idea considering the psychedelic colors in its retro print were making her dizzy again. She closed her eyes. "Of course, I'm happy he did well. It's just that I didn't expect him to do *so* well—even better than me." She sighed. "Now, Chuck officially does everything better than me."

"We both know that's not true," Audrey replied. "For once, this time Chuck put all his energies into it—"

"Even so..." Charly muttered.

"What do you mean by that?"

"Mom, Chuck isn't the only one who scored well. All of Miranda's concierge students scored at least fourteen hundred—even the ones who barely studied—or left early!" Charly shrugged. "At least, that's what Manya and Zina said."

Audrey frowned. "Were they also coached by Egan?"

"Yes. Granted, they say he was a real taskmaster—"

"Well, then, there you have it. You know as well as I do that AA students have been taught comprehensive learning techniques. Isn't that why you've spent the past four years at the school?"

"Yes. But—"

"Egan was successful in motivating them to channel their energies and skills into the test. That says a lot about his abilities as a teacher."

"Yeah...I guess." She looked away. "Why don't you ask Chuck what he thinks?"

"Okay, I will. But not at the expense of bruising his ego. Chuck worked hard for that grade. He should know we're all proud of him—you, especially."

Charly snickered. "If you say so."

"I do. He respects you more than anyone in the whole world."

Charly wondered, does he?

Of course, she already knew the answer to that. The bond between the twins had always been forged in love and loyalty.

"Okay," she murmured.

Audrey looked at her watch. "It's already noon. The others left at ten."

"On a ride?" Charly was disappointed she'd missed it. Then again, the thought of riding at breakneck speed on Mount Tam's bike trails made her want to hurl again.

"No, they aren't cycling today. They're at Lavinia's house, packing it up. I told them we'd be there as soon as you woke up."

Charly groaned again. "Do I have to go? I feel awful."

"Unfortunately, yes. It's all hands on deck." Audrey stood up. "One of Lavinia's wishes was that it be sold and the proceeds go toward establishing a scholarship endowment in her name. The house is worth close to two million dollars."

Charly's heart lurched in her chest. "Wait!… Does that mean we don't own it? *That none of us can ever live there?*"

"I know how you feel, Charly. And trust me, I feel the same way." She took Charly's hand. "Until it sells, we can go there as often as we like. And we can take whatever belongings we want to remember her by."

Charly tried to protest, but no words came out.

She was glad her mother walked out the door before she threw up again.

CHAPTER 12

*D*espite having a three-hour head start, Daniel, Chuck, and Noah had barely made a dent in the chore of cleaning out Lavinia's house.

A U-Haul truck sat in the driveway, along with Daniel's car.

Daniel was waiting for Audrey and Charly. As they walked onto the front porch, he handed each of them a small pad of Stick-It notes. Audrey's was pale pink, whereas Charly's pad was bright orange.

"Today, we're boxing up stuff to give to the Salvation Army, which will pick it up sometime next week," Daniel explained. "There are boxes in every room. If you want to hold onto something, put your name on the box, toss in anything you want, and take your filled boxes down to either of the cars. If it's too big to box up, put your name on it with a Stick-It note. Tomorrow we'll fill the U-Haul and move the bigger pieces to our house." He nodded at Audrey. "Chuck is working in the living room. And since the garden is still filled with produce, I asked Noah to pluck anything that we can take home with us. Quite frankly, I think we'll also be able to drop a few boxes of produce at the Delancey Street Mission."

"They'll appreciate it," Audrey murmured. "I guess I'll start in Lavinia's bedroom, and then I'll move on to the kitchen."

"Good." Daniel turned to Charly. "Why don't you take the two smaller upstairs bedrooms?"

Charly nodded. She was glad he didn't mention her night out clubbing. She was sure to hear enough about it from Chuck before the day was out.

The guest room was the easiest of the two smaller bedrooms to box up, so Charly started there.

Twenty minutes later, Charly had moved on to her mother's childhood bedroom.

Having played in Lavinia's house all her life, she'd been in the room more times than she could remember. Not surprisingly, her grandmother had left it like a time capsule. Its double bed was covered with a homemade quilt made by Lavinia. A few of Audrey's stuffed animals were still propped casually among the bed's mountain of throw pillows.

The posters hanging on the walls never failed to put a smile on Charly's face. Knowing that her mother was once into Alice in Chains, Metallica, and Nine Inch Nails blew her mind.

Charly made a note to roll them up. She'd have them framed and present them to Audrey on her next birthday.

Her mother's closet was a treasure trove of period clothing. But even back in the day, Audrey had a mature fashion style: slacks as opposed to acid-washed jeans; blouses, not tee shirts. There was none of the usual fashion faux pas from the teen era she'd lived through.

Actually, there were a few pieces that Charly coveted: wide-legged tan pants, a sleeveless black mock turtleneck sweater, and a raincoat with an empire waist. If any of these items were from Sienna's grandparents' store, they'd be worth a small fortune now. Although Audrey was shorter than Charly, both were slender, so maybe it would work out. She set these items aside in an empty box.

One fashion accessory that seemed a bit out of place was a pair of boots: pink Doc Martens illustrated with London icons. Her mother's other shoes were flat slippers, although there was a pair of Converse sneakers.

Because the boots were practically brand new, she put them in her take-home box as well.

The only things on the closet's upper shelf were old handbags and a cardboard box.

Charly grabbed the box and set it on the floor. One of the items inside was an Ashbury Academy yearbook from her mother's senior year.

The longest messages were scribbled along the borders of the pages showing black and white photos of her mother laughing and hugging her closest friends: Bliss, Davis, Tallulah, and Gemma—

And some guy named Jeremy.

Like the others, Jeremy's memories were relayed in a shorthand that only the writer and the recipient would understand. Whereas the other four messages were light and humorous, this Jeremy person's comments were filled with longing and regret.

My mother was a heartbreaker, Charly realized.

This unexpected revelation gave her pause. Even with

visual proof in hand, the realization that her mother was once a teenager coveted by boys seemed to knock her world off-kilter, sending it spinning in the wrong direction.

The next thing she pulled from the cardboard container was a small lacquered burlwood box.

There wasn't much inside. The box's pull-out tray was divided into six square compartments. One square contained a bracelet covered in charms. A mood ring filled another. Tiny diamond ear studs and other trinkets were placed in the other chambers.

Charly pulled out the tray to see underneath it. There were a few torn music event tickets, most from the Fillmore. Some were for Maggie's concerts.

These are collector's items, Charly thought excitedly.

There was also a strip of miniature black-and-white photos: headshots of a young man, fresh-faced, with a cocky grin. She recognized him immediately: Egan, twenty years younger, maybe more.

A heart had been drawn around his face with a red Magic Marker.

Mom had a crush on Egan!

Charly blushed at the thought.

Is it difficult for her to see him now?

No, of course not, she reasoned. Mom's an adult. She's got kids.

And a husband.

She loves Dad…

But then she saw it: the last thing in the cardboard box:

Another book—

Extracurricular.

The title page was earmarked with a ticket to some event: Egan had been interviewed at UC Berkeley about his break-out debut novel.

And he'd signed the page:

Dear Audrey,
You were the ideal fantasy.
May our reality be just as wonderful.
With all my heart,
Love, Egan

My mother—was once Egan's fantasy?
And what had he hoped was their "reality"?
Emotions roiled through Charly. she thought back at the few times she'd seen her mother and Egan together. By her nature, Audrey was always reserved. But whenever Egan was around, Charly had noticed her mother's eyes brighten and her voice took on a charged lilt.

Then again, most women seemed to appreciate Egan's charm.

Charly looked down at the ticket. Its date put it just nine months before Chuck's and her birth.

She remembered how upset her mother was when, on the first day of school, the twins had teased her about their parents' wedding day. It took place less than nine months before their birth.

Stunned by the implication, Charly leaped up from the floor. Out of the corner of her eye, she caught sight of her reflection in the dresser mirror.

Oh my God—

Is Egan our father?

The book fell from her hands, hitting the hardwood floor with a loud thunk.

From Lavinia's old bedroom, she heard her mother exclaim, "Charly? Are you okay in there?"

"Fine! Everything is…just fine!" Charly shoved the burl-wood box and the two books under the clothing in her take-home box. She then folded the box closed, wrote her name on a Stick-It note, and taped it to the box.

As quietly as she could, she tiptoed downstairs with it.

Her father's car keys lay on the foyer table. She placed the box in the far corner of his trunk.

She'd retrieve it later.

"What's this for again?" Warily, Chuck eyed the small plastic tube Charly had handed him.

"Biology class. Extra credit. For my experiment, I need a sample from you." She nodded toward Noah. "No biggie. He's given me one as well."

Noah gave Chuck a thumbs up. "But only because she gave me ten bucks."

For Charly, the bribe was worth it. There was no way she could dare ask Daniel for a saliva sample. But since half of Noah's DNA was his, if in fact the twins and Noah had different fathers, they'd know immediately.

Chuck cocked a brow. "You're not going to clone me, are you?"

Charly snorted. "Trust me, one of you is more than enough."

Chuck laughed. "Alright, but let me grab my phone. If I'm going to spill my seed, I'll need to look at some porn. I'm not a bonobo, you know—"

"Why porn…?" When the reason came to her, she punched his arm, horrified. "Not sperm, you idiot!"

"Oh..." Chuck shrugged. "Okay, then at least let me drink a couple of glasses of water." He held up the tube. "Although, it's small enough that I might be able to pee without any—"

"*Ew...no!*" She raised her hand in frustration. "Look, just give me some *saliva!*"

"Oh!... Why didn't you just say so?" He spit it into the tube until his saliva reached the fill line.

As Charly took it from him, she shuddered. Not just because he was grossing her out, but because she hated herself for following up on her sad, sick hunch about her mother's secret.

Hopefully, she was wrong.

She wouldn't dare ask her mother. Not when a DNA test was easy enough to get.

In eight to ten weeks, I'll know for sure.

She wondered if getting a sample from Egan would be as bothersome to retrieve.

Somehow, she doubted it.

Frankly, it was easier than Charly thought.

It helped that Egan was vain enough to keep a well-stocked toiletry bag in his bottom desk drawer. She'd learned about it a few months back. After his lunch shift, she'd noticed him carrying a toothbrush when strolling back into his classroom.

She'd teased him about it too. "Worried about gum disease?"

"That—and coffee breath," he'd admitted. She'd even joked that it was the same color as the one she had at home: pink.

"You're stuck with whatever colors they put in a four-pack," he insisted. "And using it here—doesn't that make me woke?"

She laughed so hard that he joined in.

Thankfully, it was in his bag. While he was out to lunch, Charly entered his classroom and swapped it out for a new identical one she'd taken from her bathroom closet.

She chided herself for her suspicions, but it was better to know for all their sakes.

At least, that's what she told herself.

CHAPTER 13

The months of January, February, and March were declared San Francisco's soggiest winter in a decade.

To Audrey's relief, it didn't help the sale of Lavinia's house.

"Don't realtors suggest that sellers frou-frou up a place before putting it on the market?" Daniel asked.

Audrey chuckled. "Exactly what do you mean by that?"

"You know…" Daniel struggled to find the right words. "They bring in nice furniture to fake the fact that someone is living there. And they make the place smell like choco-late chip cookies are baking in the oven."

Audrey shrugged. "I guess so. Maybe I'll suggest that to our realtor."

She was lying. In fact, the realtor had already recom-mended staging the house.

Audrey had told him not to bother. She dreaded the

thought of selling Lavinia's house. In fact, she wanted to buy it herself.

But doing so would mean dipping into the children's college funds—something neither she nor Daniel could do, especially now that two university tuitions would soon be staring them in the face.

Both of the twins had applied to UC Berkeley—their first choice and parents' alma mater—and UCLA, their second.

Acceptances were due in late March, as was the case with the other UC campuses. Chuck had also applied to Davis, San Diego, and Santa Cruz.

Charly had also sent applications to Stanford, Boston University, Wellesley, and USC, but she'd refused to apply for early admission. In her mind, these were fallback positions should she not get accepted to Berkeley.

In any event, at the least, Daniel and Audrey would be shelling out thirty thousand dollars per child per year unless scholarships could be wrangled from the schools.

So, even as a rental investment, hanging onto Lavinia's house was not an option.

Audrey sighed. "I'll call the realtor first thing in the morning."

"Okay, folks—listen up!" Egan scanned the faces of AA's Debate Team. "As you already know, tomorrow's debate is the last one before the state tournament. We'll be facing off against Saint Ignatius, which, like us, has a record of ten wins and no losses." He paced the floor. "We're in this fight because each of you has brought your personal best to every previous match. And"—Egan's pause warned the team to listen up; that what he had to say next was very important—"it's why, should we win our division today, I'll finally be making good on my promise of choosing our team captain—the person I feel could help us become state champions."

It has to be me. Please, God, let it be me, Charly prayed.

"But first things first. To take the division crown, we've got to win two out of tomorrow's three matches based on the questions you've researched, summarized, and drilled for all week."

Egan pointed to the whiteboard:

• *Should high schools drop football because of the potential for life-altering injuries?*

• *Is a college education necessary in this day and age?*

• *Should our political leaders be held to a higher ethical standard?*

"However, we're approaching this last match differently," Egan explained. "Each question will be the *sole domain* of one of our top three scorers. They will give pro, con, and rebuttal arguments for their questions. Their success is our success. But only one of them can lead us into the state tournament. Tomorrow will decide who that will be."

The students exchanged knowing glances. It was no secret that Chuck, Charly, and Fawn were the team's highest point scorers.

Egan scanned the room. When he found Chuck, he smiled. "Chuck, you'll do pro, con, and rebuttal on the first question," Egan declared.

Chuck's nod was accompanied by a shrug.

Since the SAT test, Chuck seemed more serious—stoic, perhaps.

I guess the test served its purpose, Egan reasoned. He's taking life more seriously.

As much as Egan had hoped for that, it also saddened him. Chuck's laugh was infectious. His sense of humor lifted the spirits of all around him. Egan never realized how much he appreciated it until now.

His gaze shifted to Fawn, who sat two seats to the right of the boy. "Fawn, you'll do the same on the second one."

She preened as she nodded, then glanced over anxiously at Chuck to gauge his response to her great luck.

The kid's yawn was hardly an acknowledgment.

I guess it's finally over between those lovebirds, Egan reasoned.

Finally, Egan turned to Charly. "The third question is all yours, kiddo." The bestowment came with a wink and a grin.

Charly felt herself blushing, but she nodded back.

Even before she found her mother's copy of *Extracurricular*, she'd already made up her mind to impress Egan so much that he'd have to make her captain.

If what she suspected about his real role in her life was true, it would mean more to her than ever.

She loved Daniel and knew he was proud of her and that he loved her too. And yet, she'd always felt the need to compete for his love.

Not that winning Egan's adoration would come any easier. She could see that already. If he suspected—or for that matter, if he already knew he was her father, he certainly didn't show it.

Charly had always scored high in Egan's Comp Lit class. But since her suspicions, she'd made a concerted effort to earn what his students jokingly called "Egan's A+++ Compliment of the Week."

They could jest, but Egan's acknowledgments were coveted nonetheless.

Fawn had worked just as hard for Egan's recognition, and bristled visibly whenever he complimented anyone else—

Especially Charly.

In Chuck's case, whereas he'd been enamored with Egan before receiving his exemplary SAT score, Chuck's attitude toward their teacher had changed. He no longer sought Egan's approval.

For that matter, he seemed to have distanced himself from Daniel too.

Even more shocking, he had totally dumped Fawn.

Chuck was now fully self-driven.

I guess that's a good thing, Charly reasoned.

For that very reason, she was glad that she hadn't revealed her suspicions about Audrey and Egan to Chuck. If the DNA test proved she was right, he'd be a victim to the same emotional turmoil that coursed through her.

Would her brother accept the test results, despite knowing it would crush Daniel?

Would he, like she, be upset with their mother keeping from them this life-changing secret?

Her guess was yes to both.

These days, Charly could barely stand looking at Audrey, let alone being around her mother. She was silent in the morning drives to school. And after school, she'd gotten adept at finagling excuses to stay away from home.

Thankfully, her loving friends indulged her. But by the concern in their voices, she knew they were worried about what she wasn't telling them.

She threw herself into the one thing she found joy in doing: working through every debate question, from every angle—not just the ones Egan had assigned her.

Charly was the undisputed star of Ashbury Academy's debate team.

Tomorrow she would prove it.

To Egan, especially.

She wondered how he'd respond to the knowledge that he was a father of two, and teenagers at that? If it turned out she was right about his relationship with their mother, she hoped that the time Egan had spent with the twins would make it easier for him to accept her love.

And hopefully, Chuck's too.

She had no doubt that Chuck's shock and awe at the revelation would mirror her own. He respected Egan. That could be the start of the bond between father and son.

Hopefully, one that would strengthen between them for the rest of their lives.

And yet, Charly worried how Daniel would take the news.

It would break his heart, she feared.

Could he ever forgive their mother for lying to him all these years?

For that matter, would Egan forgive Audrey for hiding the truth from him as well?

It would be difficult, Charly realized.

She knew this from experience. Her anxiety over the DNA test results grew with each passing week.

So did her antipathy toward her mother.

As anxious as Audrey was about Lavinia's house, she was even more concerned about Charly.

Her daughter was avoiding her, and Audrey didn't know why.

Ever since the night Charly came home drunk, she now found excuses to spend less time at home. Instead, she hid out in her friends' homes.

She never invites them here anymore, Audrey realized sadly.

She knew her daughter was competitive—especially with Chuck. Audrey wondered if his higher SAT score had shaken Charly's confidence to the point that she was now ashamed to face her family.

Was Charly finding solace in drink—or worse yet, drugs? Although pot wasn't allowed in school, it was ubiquitous with students everywhere.

Audrey prayed this wasn't the case. In the past, Charly had stayed away from it. She never saw the purpose of mind-altering substances—be they drunk, inhaled, or ingested.

If Charly was at Manya's house, Audrey avoided calling Nira to confirm it. A physician, Nira was rarely home before eight o'clock. She was also a strict parent and would wonder why Audrey was checking up on her daughter. The last thing Audrey needed was for Nira to forbid Manya from seeing Charly.

And besides, since Nira accepted the trustee board's offer to join it, the last thing Audrey wanted was anyone— even Daniel—to know she was concerned about Charly's behavior.

When Charly claimed to be at Zina or Sienna's homes, Audrey would wait an hour or two before calling the hosting mother. After small talk or gossip, she'd find an excuse to ask after the girls.

"They're fine," Gemma would insist. To prove it, she held out the phone in the girls' direction so that Audrey could hear their giggles or catch a snippet of their conversation.

Inevitably it was about their studies.

Bliss, too, always confirmed their whereabouts.

But today, after Audrey's seventh such call, Bliss bluntly asked: "Has something happened between you and Charly?"

Audrey didn't know how to answer that. Finally, she whispered, "Yes. But I don't know what."

"Oh—my dear, sweet friend!" The concern in Bliss' voice touched her deeply. "I'm sure it's nothing to worry about. I mean, let's face it. All girls go through a period of hating their moms. Last year, Sienna acted as if I was a leper." Bliss' chuckle was half-hearted at best. "Not to worry! It's just their way to prove that they're ready to… oh, I don't know. Maybe spread their wings without asking permission?"

"But… I never felt that way," Audrey admitted.

"Why would you?" Bliss exclaimed. "Lavinia never doubted you. And she never gave you any reason to doubt her either."

"Does Charly think I doubt her?" Audrey was confused. "Or does she doubt me? Bliss, what are you saying?"

"Audrey, you're asking the wrong person," Bliss explained. "Maybe it's a conversation you should have with Charly. The sooner the better too. Hey, the debate team match is tomorrow. Why don't you ask her if she'll join you for a mother-daughter dinner afterward?"

She's right, Audrey thought. Daniel would be flying

home from New York late that evening. Noah would be sleeping over at a friend's place.

"I'm sure Chuck will be fine with us ditching him. He'll probably want to hang with Fawn anyway—particularly if her parents go out that night."

"You see?" Bliss exclaimed. "Fawn is a *perfect* example of a kid who hates her parents!"

Dismayed, Audrey insisted, "But…I'm nothing like Seamus or Gretchen McCoppin!"

"No! Of course, you're not!"

Bliss' attempt to backtrack hurt more than her honesty.

She's right. It's time for Charly and me to clear the air.

CHAPTER 14

J ust as the Newark gate attendant had informed him, Daniel discovered he'd scored the last empty seat in the first-class cabin of United's six o'clock San Francisco departure.

Another lucky twist of fate: Tallulah was in the seat across the aisle from him.

"Fancy meeting you here," she exclaimed as he bent down for a kiss.

"I don't mind changing seats," the man next to Tallulah offered. "Unless you two would prefer to join the Mile High Club."

Tallulah and Daniel roared with laughter at that.

Once they were airborne, he confessed, "I wish I'd known you were going to be in town. I hate eating dinner alone."

Tallulah chuckled. "Unfortunately, when I'm here, I'm wined and dined to death—and usually at midnight." She shrugged. "Such is the life of musicians and promoters. We keep vampire hours. It's aging me quickly." As proof, she pulled a compact from her satchel and scrutinized her face for telltale evidence.

"Don't kid yourself," Daniel insisted. "You could easily take ten years off your age, and no one would guess."

Tallulah's laugh filled the cabin. "Audrey has you well-trained." Her smile faded. "Speaking of my dear, sweet friend, how is she holding up, anyway?"

"I won't lie. Lavinia's death affected her deeply. Me and the children as well." Daniel hesitated. "I was sorry to hear Maggie took it hard too."

"Maggie always joked that she'd flame out first, what with all the drugs she'd ingested." Tallulah sighed. "I truly believe it never occurred to her that Lavinia might not always be there for her. Lavinia was her rock." She attempted a smile. "I'm glad Audrey agreed to be on the search committee."

"Audrey wouldn't have it any other way. Lavinia's legacy is the school. She insists on safeguarding it." Daniel grimaced. "Unfortunately, Gretchen McCoppin is on it, too —and she's not making it easy for her. What with your role in chairing AA's anniversary gala too, I'm just glad you're also there on the board's behalf. Between the two of you, Gretchen can't do too much damage."

Tallulah nodded. "The gala is on a glide path now. Bliss is perfectly capable of wrapping up any loose ends. Replacing Lavinia with the right person is the priority now."

"I couldn't agree more." Daniel attempted a smile. "The only thing that's raised Audrey's spirits is Chuck's SAT score. Somehow he managed to pull off fifteen-twenty-two."

Tallulah frowned. "That's…interesting."

Daniel laughed, "I know. Hard to believe, isn't it?"

"No more than Quest pulling off fourteen-eleven. Jokingly, I asked him if he'd found some cheat sheet. He said no. That Egan had spent a long time drilling him on the basics. Still..." Tallulah shook her head. "Then he told me Jammerhead had signed him up for Miranda's concierge counseling program, which meant he could take as long as he wanted to answer questions. Quest said that when he went to her office to sign off on his application, he noticed she plumped it up with stuff he'd never done—like rowing crew and volunteering at some non-profit group he'd never heard of. When Quest questioned Miranda about it, she blew up at him. Told him that Jammerhead had paid her a pretty penny to quote-unquote assure that he got into a prestigious business music program." She frowned.

"How long ago was this?"

"Quest told me right as I was leaving for Manhattan."

"Have you asked Jammerhead about it?"

"He's on the road." Tallulah scowled. "Even hearing what little Quest knew, I quickly figured out it's not the sort of discussion one should have over the phone."

"You're right about that—especially if what Miranda has done involves bribery and fraud."

"Oh, my God!" Tallulah muttered. Perplexed, she slunk down in her seat. "The last thing we need is a scandal—especially one that could land Jammerhead in jail!"

"The school doesn't need this sort of headache either," Daniel pointed out. "Listen, Tallulah, give me a dollar."

Startled, she stammered, "What for?"

"Just do it," he ordered.

She reached into her satchel and pulled out a single bill.

Daniel pocketed it. "You've just retained me as your lawyer. That way, if Jammerhead has done anything illegal that he hadn't previously divulged to you, I've got your back."

"Thanks, Daniel." Stony eyed, she stared straight ahead. "So, what's our next move, counselor?"

"Don't say anything yet to anyone. I'll do a little background research on Ms. D'Arcy."

Tallulah nodded. "One thing we know: Miranda is an alumnus. And, supposedly, she built a business based on the success of her so-called college counseling skills."

"Both of which got her to sidestep any serious employment vetting—at least where Lavinia was concerned," Daniel replied. "Considering how competitive college is these days, it makes sense that she's playing with a loaded deck. I suspect she's bribing a few university staffers. Now, the big question is whether her clients know this is going on."

"Considering that they include Seamus, Jess, and Warner, my guess is yes."

"No wonder they pushed so hard to have her replace Lavinia," Daniel reasoned. "What better way to cover their tracks? For now, anyway."

"If what you suspect is right, Quest is going to be crushed when the shit hits the fan." Tallulah's voice trembled. "I guess Jammerhead is so desperate that Quest should be something more than just a musician. Why can't parents—my husband included—just let their kids live their lives?"

Fawn looked around Ashbury Academy's auditorium. It was a full house. Pride in this year's Debate Eight was sky-high.

One more reason she wanted to win the title of debate team captain.

But first, she'd have to impress Egan, which meant earning the best score in today's match.

Her plan was simple: memorize her arguments perfectly. Make eye contact with the judges. Speak with authority, but with brevity as well.

And most importantly, find some way to trip up Charly, who would also be doing all of the above.

Granted, even if her scheme worked, there was an outside chance that Egan would bestow it to Chuck.

That would undoubtedly present a conundrum.

Ever since they got back their SAT results, Chuck had been distant to her.

He no longer begged to spend time with her.

Worse yet, he found excuses to avoid her.

She was sure his bitch of a sister had something to do with that.

Miffed at Chuck's desertion, Fawn initiated the one failsafe ploy women had been using since Eve wrapped herself in live snakeskin: she flirted.

Hugo was the lucky guy, and didn't he just know it.

To her dismay, Chuck didn't seem to care.

Fawn's Hail Mary pass was delivered in a hand-written, scented note left in Chuck's locker:

I don't know why you hate me all of a sudden. At least have the courage to talk to me about it. My jailers will be out tonight. How about my place, tonight, after the match?

xoxoxoxox Fawn

She planned the best make-up session ever.

It would begin with a little move she'd perfected on her Cheerfully Yours website. She called it "Cherry Pie."

When she debuted it just last week, the clicks were astronomical, and new sign-ups went through the roof.

Best yet, the bid on the rainbow-hued spankies she'd worn during the erotic cheerleading routine brought in the highest bid in the site's history: an incredible ten thousand dollars.

Tucked into the spankies was a personalized note for the winner, someone who went by the nickname of BigBadDaddy:

> *Sweet dreams, BigBadDaddy!*
> *XOXOXOX!*
> *—Miss Cheer Fully*

And should, for some unfathomable reason, Egan choose Chuck as captain, Fawn had no doubt that a double-dip of Cherry Pie would convince him to pass on the honor and suggest bestowing it on her instead.

This would peeve Charly to no end.

More importantly, it would shock Seamus into realizing she wasn't a bimbo after all.

Fawn loved the thought that becoming debate team captain would buoy his hopes about her chances for getting into Yale. She couldn't wait to say no to all the acceptances. That would teach Seamus a lesson for blowing her right to try for it on her own.

Until then, she'd have to play the good girl until her college acceptances rolled in. She had no doubt they would, and in droves. The package Miranda had created for Fawn, sent to the top ten universities touted on *US News & World Report*, had all the bells and whistles. Besides her sky-high SAT score, Miranda had doctored some of Fawn's previous grades.

She'd even faked Fawn's participation in some supposedly international non-profit club called Best Face Forward. It was supposed to be like 4-H, but instead of pretending to be farmers, the members were supposed to do good deeds for the needy.

As if we're some sort of bleeding-heart losers, Fawn scoffed.

The catch was, there really wasn't such a club.

Fawn realized this when Miranda insisted she wear a tee shirt with the organization's logo and then marched Fawn out onto a nearby street corner to take a picture of her handing sandwiches to a couple of homeless guys.

But just as Miranda shot the picture, one of the men pinched Fawn's ass. Fawn slapped his face so hard that the dirty old codger lost a tooth.

When he howled for the cops, Miranda shut him up with a fifty-dollar bill.

"That's going on Seamus' bill," Miranda warned Fawn.

"Oh, yeah? Then I'll tell him about your so-called non-profit," the girl retorted.

"And I'll tell him about your whore-tart website," Miranda shot back.

Noting Fawn's blush, Miranda added: "And by the way, that lecher bait goes dark the moment you get home. Should any of the college recruiters find out about it, all of your parents' money for this little endeavor goes up in smoke!"

"Yeah, okay, sure," Fawn pouted. *Like hell, I will!*

The money was too good.

And besides, the more it made for her, the quicker she could leave Seamus and Gretchen in her rearview mirror.

First things first: make Seamus regret he'd ever doubted her.

So yes, tonight was important. She just had to make team captain.

Fawn watched as her parents made their entrance. She'd reserved seats for them next to Audrey Thorpe just because she knew they despised each other.

Served them all right.

***

The judges selected for the debate match—two women and one man, all retired lawyers—were a solemn bunch.

As was the tradition, the debaters shook each judge's hand before taking their podiums.

Chuck's match was first. He considered himself lucky that he drew the con argument on the question as to whether football should be abolished from school sports.

It allowed him to expound eloquently on football's role in American culture: how it brought communities together and played an integral role in America's civil rights history.

"Football is as American as apple pie," he concluded.

He won a comfortable victory over his opponent.

Usually, when Chuck won at anything, his exuberance never seemed to fail him. This time, though, he nodded with a slim grimace as he left the podium.

He'd spent the last couple of months in a haze of doubt.

It had started when Fawn declared that Egan had nudged their SAT tests above the 1400-score sweet spot.

And that he'd done so at Miranda's behest. Apparently, it was something she did for all her concierge clients—for the right price.

He found it hard to believe Egan was on the take. At least, not from the way he'd worked so hard with Chuck to make sure he'd succeed on the test.

Miranda must be one great lay, Chuck thought. What other reason was there? Besides, he'd seen the way she simpered and preened whenever Egan was around.

Dad pushed hard for me to talk to Miranda. I should come right out and ask Dad if Fawn is right, Chuck thought.

But he quickly nixed that idea. He was afraid that his father would confirm his worse suspicions: that Daniel acted out of desperation because he'd been unsure of Chuck's ability to bring his A-game to the test.

The thought cut him to the quick.

Upon hearing Fawn's claim, Chuck's shock turned to anger. In time, it softened to sullen bitterness.

Had it not rained so hard all winter, Chuck would have come up with excuses for why he was no longer interested in the family's Saturday bike treks.

Lately, Chuck had been tempted to tell his mother his suspicions, but he couldn't stand the thought of upsetting her.

Not so soon after Lavinia's death.

Instead, he'd prove his father wrong.

It would start with winning the debate team captainship.

Too bad his father had missed seeing his son prove him wrong.

My turn, Fawn thought.

And she was ready to win her match. She'd felt she'd

drawn a great question: whether college still was necessary in this day and age. She sauntered up to the judges' table with a beaming smile.

But as she shook the male judge's hand, she noticed he held it too firmly and for too long. She wondered why he was staring at her. She figured it out when he murmured, "Win one for Big Bad Daddy."

Oh....

Shit.

Suddenly, she couldn't breathe. It was as if her whole world was closing in on her. Her gaze went from her judge who gave her a broad wink, to her father—

Whose wink was even broader.

Shit, shit, shit!

Fawn drew the con argument.

She started out with a stutter, then willed herself to take control. But despite having memorized her argument and practicing it for an hour, she couldn't remember any of it.

There was nothing she could do but wing it.

She opened with some riff about lazy students who were only in school to party on their parents' dime. She then reeled into a speech about all the millionaires who, through sheer pluck and ingenuity, made their fortunes without a college degree. She tossed in survival of the fittest, charisma, karma, and good luck—none of which, she claimed, came out of a classroom.

Fawn knew she should be making eye contact with the judges, but if she dared to look at Big Bad Daddy, she knew she'd melt into a puddle of insecurity.

When the match came to an end, this decision counted against her.

Except with one judge, who gave her a perfect score.

After the match was decided, Fawn rushed out of the auditorium. She was too ashamed to face any of the men in her life: not Seamus.

Not Egan.

And certainly not Chuck.

The second she got home, she vowed, I'm deleting Big Bad Daddy's accounts.

———

As Charly had hoped, she drew the pro argument on her match question: whether political leaders should be held to a higher ethical standard.

Using the threads of wisdom sewn into the fabric of the U.S. Constitution, she began with a cautionary tale of executive power. Then, as if cross-stitching squares in a quilt, Charly presented historical examples of self-sacrifice during times of historical unrest.

The seamless pattern of selflessness, honor, and duty unfurled in her closing argument brought the audience to its feet.

On the heels of that, her competitor's argument unraveled like pantyhose.

Her score was the highest of both teams.

It won Ashbury Academy the district title.

———

The audience broke out in pandemonium.

Charly was swallowed up in the team's group hug.

Finally, the others peeled away, leaving her with Chuck's arm around her shoulders.

Egan walked up to them. As he shook her hand, he murmured, "Congratulations, Captain...McKittridge."

She was struck by the way he grimaced and hesitated when saying her last name.

Does he know about us?

How she ached to ask him.

A moment later, Audrey was at their side. As she nodded to Egan, Charly watched his face closely for any sign of—

Of what? Sadness? Longing? Regret?

His benign grin betrayed nothing.

When Audrey put her arm around Charly's waist, the girl shrugged it off. Obviously dismayed at the rejection, Audrey's smile faltered. Still, she insisted, "We should celebrate. Just the two of us. Somewhere special! How about Gary Danko?"

"I'm too tired," Charly muttered stiffly. "Let's just go home."

Bemused, Egan declared, "You're kidding, right? You've wanted the captainship since I mentioned it! You've earned it fair and square. And Danko's? Are you really going to turn down that tasting menu? Take her up on the offer, Charly! You've earned it."

"But...I really don't want to." Charly turned to Chuck, but he was too caught up in his own thoughts to cipher her silent plea for help.

Noting her concern, Egan replied, "Don't worry about your brother. I'll buy him a burger. Besides, I need to pick his brain on our upcoming strategy for the state tournament."

Why does Egan want to eat with Chuck?

Why not me?

Chuck seemed just as surprised by the offer—and just as perplexed.

"That's very kind of you, Egan." The relief in Audrey's voice put a grin on Egan's face.

This was not lost on Charly.

Neither was the look on Egan's face: as if Charly had somehow disappointed him.

If only she could explain why.

CHAPTER 15

"Two burgers—and two Cloud Covers on tap."

Egan ignored the waitress' sly wink. She usually flirted with him, but now was not the time to flirt back.

Not with his son in tow.

When she walked off, Egan realized she may have not been coming onto him at all. "Jeez, I forgot...you're not twenty-one yet!"

"She doesn't know that. And besides, she likes you." By his tone, he didn't find that funny or for that matter, concerning.

"I guess it's not as if you haven't had a beer or two."

"You were a teenager once," Chuck countered. "What do you think?"

"I did," Egan admitted. "I usually snuck one out of my dad's six-packs. Nothing like the wild parties you AA kids throw."

Chuck snickered. "I don't throw them. I just attend them."

"College will be even more of that," Egan assured him.

"If I get there," Chuck muttered.

"You really are the full package, Chuck. You're personable. You're athletic. And you pulled your grades up. Your SAT was nothing to sneeze at." Egan tossed their menus aside. "For you, college is just the first step. You can do anything you set your mind on."

Chuck shrugged. "I may not go."

"Why would you say that?" Egan's eyes opened wide with surprise.

"Because I didn't earn it." The boy turned to stare at one of the big-screen monitors over the bar. A Warriors game was playing, muted.

Egan frowned. "What do you mean by that?"

"Fawn told me…she says you doctored our SAT scores so that we'd make at least fourteen-hundred." Chuck leaned across the table. He locked eyes with Egan. "Is that true?"

Egan never thought he'd have to face his son and answer that question.

At least, now I can answer truthfully.

"I swear to you, Chuck, on my life—*you earned your SAT score on your own.*"

Chuck's face was like an open book in which its pages, illustrated with the boy's emotions, were being flipped at breakneck speed. Doubt made way for wariness, which was replaced by comprehension, then relief, and finally jubilation. "I knew it! What she said—it was just too ridiculous!" His head shook, incredulous. "I mean like just because her dad doesn't believe in her, doesn't mean mine doesn't believe in me, right?"

"Your father…he will always believe in you. He will

always be there for you." Egan spoke so softly that Chuck leaned in to hear him.

At that very moment, their waitress appeared with their meal on a tray. But when she placed their beers on the table, Egan waved them away. "We've changed our minds. We'll have water instead."

After she left, Chuck burst out laughing. "Dude... you're not mad because I accused you of doing something fishy, are you?"

"No, not in the least. To be honest, I wouldn't have had it any other way. I'd feel bad if you didn't trust me, and I didn't know why." Egan pointed to the burgers in front of them. "Let's dig in."

Even before the second dish of Audrey and Charly's three-course tasting menu came to their table, their conversation had gone off the rails.

For the life of her, Audrey couldn't understand why.

On the way over to the restaurant, Charly's answers to Audrey's questions about upcoming school events, her teammates, and their prep for the forthcoming tournament were clipped at best.

The girl said nothing at all during their short wait to be seated and instead busied herself by roaming through text messages.

By the time the first course was served, Audrey was upset enough to ask, "Charly, you seem so...so distant. Is it because you're missing Lavinia?"

This has nothing to do with Lavinia.

This is all on you.

Guess again. Keep guessing. But trust me—

You'll never guess in a million years.

Unless you have a guilty conscience.

For over two months, Charly had made a concerted effort to avoid looking at Audrey. She was too afraid that her emotions would give her away.

But now that they were face to face across the restaurant table, everything—the elegant setting, even the diorama of San Francisco Bay playing out in the large picture window beside them to a cacophony of fog horns —receded into nothingness.

All she saw was her mother—pensive, hopeful, wary.

No—she is scared.

At that moment, Charly realized she'd never really seen her mother as an ordinary person. She'd always had her mother on a pedestal. Audrey Thorpe: a loving mother, adoring wife, perfect daughter, and loyal friend.

Audrey Thorpe, whom others counted on to pick up the slack; to come to the rescue.

To always do the right thing.

Audrey Thorpe, of whom so much was expected, but who never anticipated anything in return.

But that wasn't Audrey at all.

Once, Audrey Thorpe had been a seventeen-year-old girl who apparently had a crush on her cute, young, charismatic teacher. The two-inch-square photo of Egan marked with a heart was proof of that.

And once, Egan had been smitten with her too. The inscription in Audrey's copy of *Extracurricular* spoke volumes to that.

If they'd had a liaison, and if the result of it had been

Charly and Chuck, and if for any reason Audrey didn't want to share that with him, surely the turmoil it had caused her had been tremendous.

And Egan's return to Ashbury Academy would be reason enough for each of the emotions now writ large on her mother's face.

If Charly were to ask Audrey all of this point-blank—right here, right now—would her mother answer her truthfully?

She hoped so, but now she wasn't sure.

After all, Audrey was just like everyone else: human.

Charly reached across the table. Taking her mother's hand, she murmured, "Yes, Mom. I miss Lavinia with all my heart. I wish she were here with us now."

Audrey nodded. Then, in unison, they turned and gazed out at the mist-kissed bay.

The DNA test results will arrive any week now, Charly reasoned. Until then, she would just have to pretend that everything was fine and dandy.

CHAPTER 16

"So, how do you feel about Netflix?" Davis' call to Egan came just as he was about to enter the school.

It wasn't the best time to take a call. The final first-class bell would ring at any moment, and at noon, the Debate Eight was driving down to Los Angeles for the state tournament, and there was still a lot of prep work Egan had to do before they departed.

To make matters worse, he'd just heard from Cornell. He had to bow out as the second chaperone because of a ruptured molar.

Egan would have to find a replacement quickly. He'd text the kids to put in calls for a parent volunteer.

At a loss for words, very cautiously, Egan declared, "Well, I was never a big *BoJack Horseman* fan, if that's what you're asking, Davis. But I enjoy *Living with Yourself*. I'm big on dark humor—"

Davis groaned. "I'm not asking you for a program

critique. I'm trying to tell you that the network's suits flipped over my pitch to turn it into a limited series."

Jesus, he did it. Extracurricular *will be on TV…*

"Expect a call from Amy Sorenson. She's with ICA—International Creative Agency, one of the talent handlers I mentioned. I think you'll like her. If so, let me know, and I'll cc my option contract to both of you so that she can go over it with a fine-tooth comb. I'll release the option as soon as you sign on the dotted line."

"Great, then let 'er rip." Egan knew just how he'd use the funds: for Chuck and Charly.

Davis added, "Hey, listen. To up your fee, how do you feel about taking the first stab at the pilot script? I want to keep your voice in the show as much as possible, and I find that's usually the best way to do it."

"*Me?*… Sure, I guess."

"Great. I'll send a separate contract for that as well. No guarantees that everything in it will make it all the way to final draft or that I won't need to bring in a script doctor to massage it in places, but at least that will assure you a partial screenwriting credit. And as far as your commitment to the school, I know you'll be tied up through May, but don't worry. We have some breathing room. I'll just need a first draft by mid-August at the latest. I'll send you a care package with my notes on how I see the book breaking down into ten episodes. I'll also forward a few scripts from other series with similar arcs, and a link to the scriptwriting app you should use, so that you get the format down pat. If you could also watch the shows, you'll get a better idea of how they turned out in post-production."

"Many thanks, Davis. I'll be on the lookout for all of this."

AA's bell tower chimed the first-class warning.

Davis must have heard it too because he added, "I guess I should let you go. And hey, leave the bell tower scene in the script, okay? It wouldn't be AA—or *Extracurricular*—without it."

"Not to worry, it'll be in there."

Egan paused in front of the quad and stared up at the bell tower.

Thank you, Lavinia.

The first thing Egan did when he got to his office was write his resignation letter.

It said, simply:

> ***Dear Miranda,***
> ***Find someone else to abuse. I quit.***
> ***—Egan***

He stuck it in his pocket as if it were a talisman.

Egan would turn it in as soon as he returned from the debate tournament.

"I just got a text from Chuck." Audrey's tone worried Daniel.

He'd just walked into his office when his cell rang. What could have happened in the half-hour since he left the house? "I'm sitting down. What did he do this time?"

"Thankfully, nothing. But...the twins need a favor. Debate Team is down one chaperone."

Daniel snickered. "Are you implying that I should fill in?"

"Frankly, yes. Every other parent has begged off."

"You too?"

"The search committee has two interviews scheduled this morning and two more for Saturday, so yes. Unless you'd rather swap Debate Tournament for finding Lavinia's replacement—"

"I guess the debate team is the lesser of two evils. Okay, yeah, text Chuck that I'm in."

He'd just hung up from her when his phone buzzed again. The caller ID showed it was one of the private detectives used by his firm: Francesca Upton.

"That was quick," Daniel declared.

"Your subject—this Miranda D'Arcy—is what we shamuses call a 'scorched earth personality,'" Francesca retorted.

"I take it that means I probably won't like what I hear." He sighed. "Okay, give me the highlights."

"The last school she worked at was Bobbitt-Hennings Prep in LA, in the position of a college counselor. When a parent reported that another had boasted she'd followed through on a guarantee to secure admission to a prestigious university, Miranda was not so politely asked to vacate the position."

"I would imagine that's just part of her sales pitch. Where's the beef in that?"

"Apparently, the student in question was a dullard who just so happened to ace his SATs and get onto the university's crew team despite having a deathly fear of water. As it turns out, to make the point, his loudmouth parent felt compelled to name a few others who'd paid dearly for Miranda's bag of tricks. At that point, the school's trustee board figured she was too hot to handle and paid her a settlement to go away."

"Can you get me a list of the trustees' names?"

"I just texted it to you."

Daniel took a moment to scan it. "I've got an old classmate who's a partner at a law firm with one of these guys —Robert Edelson."

"Do you want me to follow up with your friend?"

"No, I'll do it. But see what you can find out about the loudmouth parent."

"On it," Francesca assured him.

Daniel's old acquaintance at Edelson's law firm, Terrence Owen, was out of town, litigating a case for an East Coast client. But Terry's assistant assured Daniel that she'd relay the message and its urgency the moment he called in.

Terry didn't call until just after eleven, Pacific Time.

When Daniel explained the purpose of the call, Terry didn't respond for so long that Daniel assumed they had been disconnected. Finally, he replied, "A few months ago, Rob asked to be bought out of the partnership. The other partner and I thought it was odd. He's still in his forties and healthy as an ox. His wife and kids are also in good health. Right before the buyout, a couple of FBI agents showed up, asking to see him."

"Interesting. Was it about a client?"

"Frankly, no one knows what it was about. He never said, and his assistant didn't sit in on it. I was curious enough to ask a buddy in the FBI's LA office. He told me he could say nothing about an ongoing investigation, but that the agents involved were from the San Francisco office."

Since Miranda is up here and she may be involved, that would make sense, Daniel reasoned.

"Thanks, Terry. You've been a big help."

"If you find out something interesting, don't hesitate to call back." There was no levity in Terry's request.

"I take it that Rob's buyout is still being negotiated?"

"Yes. And, frankly, if he's jumping ship for some reason that may later reflect on the firm, we'd like to close negotiations sooner than later."

"I hear you. I'll get back to you."

Had Chuck not been scheduled to pitch when Ashbury Academy's baseball team played Marin Catholic High School's some three years ago, Daniel would never have found himself in a bleacher seat next to Vance Melamed.

It was the last game of the season, and both men had arrived late. The overflow bleacher was a mix of families rooting for both teams.

As it turned out, Vance's son was the opposing pitcher.

Between shouts and cheers for their respective teams, the two men had struck up a conversation. Although Daniel's practice was corporate as opposed to criminal litigation, the fact that one of them was in law and the other in law enforcement gave them common ground.

When Daniel had mentioned he was on AA's trustee board, Vance cocked a brow. "Then, you know Darius Calder."

Daniel chuckled. "I would imagine you know him too."

"You guessed right."

"He's on the board because his wife is an alumnus, and his daughter is a student there."

At that point, an MC batter hit a double. Like others cheering on the team, Vance stood up and cheered.

But when he sat back down, he pulled a business card from his wallet and handed it to Daniel. "Just in case," he said.

Daniel had stuck the card where such random things were kept: the top righthand drawer of his desk.

He pulled it out now.

"So, how's your son's fastball these days?" That's how Vance assured Daniel he remembered him.

"Still going strong. But I'm happy he no longer has to rely on it for a college scholarship. He did more than okay on his SATs, and he seems to be pulling up his grades."

"That's...*nice.*" Vance paused before adding: "I guess AA's college counselor is doing her job. A real miracle worker."

Her job?

Miracle worker...

Daniel took the hint: Miranda was being investigated.

Vance chuckled. "So...is this a social call?"

Daniel didn't know how to answer that.

He's great, Audrey thought.

No—he's perfect.

If Lavinia were here, she'd think so too.

The Head of School candidate, Frank Michaelson, hailed from a prep school in a small Massachusetts town. He'd come with glowing letters from a decade's worth of the school's parents, faculty, and students. The school had won numerous scholastic and academic awards. Eighty percent of its students had gone on to college, sixty-eight percent of whom had been accepted to their first-choice schools.

Besides Audrey and Tallulah, Gretchen and Nira were also on the search committee, as was Odette.

Frank shook everyone's hand before walking out the door.

"He's ideal," Tallulah murmured.

"I was just thinking the same thing," Odette declared.

Gretchen shivered. "Hardly! He has no charisma! I can't see him as a leader for the students, let alone the teachers—"

"As the only teacher representative here, let me assure you I found him *scintillating*," Odette huffed.

"That's because you're…well, you're *old school*." Gretchen sniffed.

"*Merde*," Odette muttered.

"I speak French, *mademoiselle*! I know what that means!"

"Well, in that case, you'll also know what I mean when I say '*Votre approche à cette tâche est des conneries—*"

Gretchen leaped up. "How dare you call me '*des conneries*'!"

Odette shrugged. "If the *chaussure* fits—"

"Ladies, please!" Audrey shouted. This was the fifth candidate in a very long day. Audrey rubbed her temples. "The reason we are using scorecards is for this very purpose: to quantifiably assess the candidates. Any further notes you have on your observations are to be added in the comment section. *Comprendre?*"

Both women glowered at the other.

Audrey groaned. Turning to Nira, she asked, "What did you think of him?"

Nira frowned. Her glance went from Gretchen to Odette then back again. "I...could see how he might appear milquetoast to some parents."

"In other words, you're siding with Gretchen," Tallulah muttered. "Why am I not surprised?"

Audrey was literally saved by the bell—in this case, her phone's ring tone.

It was Daniel.

"I have to take this. And considering this was the last interview of the day, we may as well adjourn until Saturday."

As the others filed out, she answered the call. "If only you'd called five minutes sooner, I could have avoided a French name-calling contest."

"Sorry. Hey, listen. I won't be able to chaperone the debate team."

"But—they're counting on you!" Audrey exclaimed.

"Something big just came up. If you care to go in my stead, I'll be glad to bach it this weekend with Noah."

"But...don't you want to be there for the twins?"

"Of course I do!" Daniel sounded impatient.

And tired.

And discouraged. "But something important just got put on my plate. It's...unavoidable."

Two nights out of town with Egan.

It would be torture for both of them, albeit for different reasons. Audrey hated the thought that he'd be mooning after her in front of the twins.

"Got it." She tried for nonchalance but knew she'd failed miserably.

Without a preface or notes, she texted him the info on Saturday's interviewees. He could figure out the rest on his own.

"You're working late." Daniel hadn't bothered to knock on Miranda's door.

Entitled prick.

But aren't they all?

Annoyed, Miranda glanced up at the wall clock. It was almost six o'clock.

It had been a hell of a long day—and far from over.

All the teachers do is complain, she thought. Admittedly, not as much as the damn parents. All they think about is one-upping their besties with whatever they can get out of me for their damn brats!

Frankly, the school was a daily shit show. She had been a fool to let Seamus talk her into even the interim Head of School position—and taking on two more concierge parents, since the knew the Feds would be tickled pink about it.

Instead of dealing with the ongoing headache of the AA universe, she should have been planning her getaway.

The crap was going to hit the fan any day now.

The moment the acceptances came in.

When they did, she needed to be as far away as possible.

Not that she could say that to Daniel.

She stifled a groan as she muttered, "So, what can I do for you, Mr. McKittridge?"

"You can leave. *Right now.* Before the roof caves in on Ashbury Academy."

What is he—a mind reader?

Miranda sputtered, "I beg your pardon?"

Daniel came right up to the desk. But he didn't sit down in either of the two chairs opposite it. He stood in front of her. "I know what you're doing, Miranda. It's the same game that got you dismissed from Bobbitt-Hennings."

Miranda sat back. She couldn't help it—she had to smile.

"Well, well, well! Someone in this school has done a little homework." She snickered. "Lavinia would have hated that. Not at all 'hands-on' learning."

"How many parents did you rope into your scheme?"

"Does it matter?"

"It will when the roof caves in on them—and their children."

Miranda smirked. "If you must know, I made dreams come true for nine AA students, including Hugo, Fawn, Buck—"

"Not surprising," Daniel muttered.

"As well as Manya, Quest, and Zina," Miranda added.

He winced at the names of his children's friends. "I'm sure they all made it worth your while."

She leaned forward. "It's the only reason I'm here."

"And Seamus' full-court press will assure you lots of victims for years to come. Let me guess—he'll be skimming off the top."

"Yes, that's the game plan. He's generously offered to manage AA's various endowments so that they reach their full potential."

"Not if I can help it. I'm turning you in, Miranda—to the FBI."

Her laughter filled the room. "No, you won't, Daniel."

"Try me." He took out his phone.

"You won't because you can't practice law behind bars. And visiting rights are very strict for the sort of crimes you'll be charged with committing."

She stifled a giggle when the color drained from his face. "What the hell do you mean by that?"

"The chair you sponsored—for Egan Gable? The funds went to pay for Chuck's concierge fee."

"*What?*… How could that be?"

Miranda shrugged. "A little financial sleight of hand. Your funds went into one bank account as opposed to another. And of course, there was a bit of paperwork to back it up—with your signature on it." She smiled. "Not to worry! Remember? Chuck passed with flying colors! Of course, it meant that Egan had to jigger the lad's SAT test to make him look as intelligent as he is handsome, athletic, and…erudite." Miranda laughed raucously. "All the more reason we should both forget this conversation—until I say otherwise. Shall we?"

"I'm a lawyer—an officer of the court! I can't turn a blind eye to all of this."

Noting his crestfallen face, she smirked, "Don't be ridiculous. We only see and hear what we want. Like that last compliment I just gave Chuck. For a parent who has always insisted on honesty, didn't you find it a bit over the top? I mean, let's just call your son what he really is: *a smart ass.*"

Angrily, he took two steps toward her.

Miranda cocked a brow. "And then there's Audrey's past with Egan."

Daniel stopped cold. "What are you talking about?"

"Trust me, they were much more than student and teacher. And let me tell you, that flame never went out, as you can see for yourself." She clicked onto her phone and held it out to him so that he could see what was on it:

A video of Egan and Audrey. They were alone in the

school's reception area. She was leaning into him as he stroked her hair.

For once, Daniel's silence had nothing to do with his temperament, but his grief.

"I take it we have a deal?" Miranda asked.

He stalked out of the office without answering.

Her cackle followed him down the hall.

I have to know if it's true, Daniel realized.

But first things first.

The mother of Noah's best friend was totally open to the idea of a sleep-over. "Why should I mind? My God, you and Audrey have covered for me more times than I can remember, so go for it. You lovebirds deserve an out of town getaway."

He had no answer for that. He couldn't even admit to himself that the only reason he'd be catching the next flight to LAX was to check up on his wife—

And the man who may have put his family in legal jeopardy.

His next call was to Vance Melamed. "I'm sorry to call you so late, but after our call earlier today, I needed confirmation before reporting something I feel falls in your jurisdiction."

Vance paused before asking, "What, exactly?"

"If you need proof that Miranda D'Arcy may be cheating to get her clients' children into certain colleges, I think I can verify it for you."

"Yes, anything you can bring forward will be useful, Daniel. Why don't we meet on Monday, say at noon, at my office?" He chuckled, then added, "You did the right thing."

After Melamed hung up, he turned to the others in his office: Lionel, SallyAnne, and Riley. "I assume you were able to catch the audio on his conversation with Maleficent?"

SallyAnne smothered a grin. Lately, she'd noticed that Melamed had been calling Miranda by the nickname he'd once forbidden.

"Whenever she doesn't want us listening in, she leaves her phone in another room. I guess she didn't figure we'd tap Daniel's phone, which worked in his favor: it allowed him to get her to admit she shifted those funds in his name from the school's bank account to one of her offshore stashes," Lionel replied.

"We can now add embezzlement to Miranda's rap sheet," SallyAnne added.

"Now that we know Daniel is clean, should we cancel his surveillance?" Riley asked.

"Not yet," Melamed answered. "As angry as he is, he'll certainly confront Egan on what he knows about Miranda's activities. Who knows what he'll get Egan to confess to?"

"You mean, like the fact that Egan has never gotten over Daniel's wife?" Riley declared.

Hearing that, SallyAnne stared triumphantly at Lionel until he blushed.

"Yeah, that too," Melamed chuckled. "Ain't love grand?"

CHAPTER 17

Upon hearing from Chuck that Daniel had offered to chaperone the Debate Eight during the tournament, Egan had resolved himself to be civil and gracious to Audrey's husband, despite his suspicions about Miranda's payoff.

But at noon, it was Audrey who pulled up in the SUV that Daniel used for the family's bike trips: a Toyota Sequoia.

Egan's heart did a backflip.

"Daniel had an office emergency." Avoiding his gaze, she added, "I assume the sooner we load the kids into the cars, the sooner we'll get out of Bay Area traffic."

He nodded. Turning to the debaters, he exclaimed, "Okay, team, wagon ho! Choose your rides."

Since there were only three boys—Chuck, Quest, and Hugo—Fawn decided to ride with the boys in Egan's rented mini-van.

The other girls piled in with Audrey.

The event that was to be the pinnacle of Charly's senior year had just turned into a nightmare.

When Chuck had told Charly he'd reached out to their parents to substitute for Cornell, she'd bitten her tongue to keep from groaning aloud. With what she suspected, it was hard enough being around Audrey and Daniel. The last thing she needed was to have one of them smiling benignly at her as she walked onto the tournament stage.

Chuck later reported that Daniel had agreed to go. As anxious as that notion made her, she was fascinated at the prospect of watching him interact with Egan. Daniel had been gracious in underwriting Egan's chair. At the debate matches Daniel had attended, they were friendly enough with each other. This gave her hope that her assumption regarding her paternity would prove false. That Egan's inscription in Audrey's copy of *Extracurricular* was no more than a casual flirtation.

But now that Audrey was here instead, Charly almost fainted. She'd forced herself to dam up her fears about her mother's past until the DNA test results were in. But should Audrey or Egan show even an inkling of desire for the other, any respect she had for the lovelorn would release the torrent of revulsion barely contained in Charly's heart, washing away the promise she'd made to herself —to give her mother the benefit of the doubt.

Thank goodness the chatter of her friends shielded her desperate silence.

When they hit the halfway mark of the journey, both cars stopped for gas.

Egan suggested that the passengers change places. The girls were fine with that. Audrey figured they found it easier gossiping in Egan's presence as opposed to hers since he knew all the players in the perennial drama that was Ashbury Academy.

She was relieved when Chuck rode shotgun as opposed to crawling into the back seat with Fawn.

Obviously miffed at his choice, Fawn pulled Hugo into the far-backseat with her.

Quest groaned, "Can't you two wait until we get to the hotel?"

Audrey glanced over at Chuck in time to catch his scowl.

The tediously interminable trip just got even longer.

The caravan arrived at the Los Angeles hotel just after eight that evening.

Despite the two baskets of healthy snacks that Audrey had brought along for the ride—water bottles, apples, bananas, power bars, dried cranberries, and raisins—by then, everyone was famished.

"We'll check in first. Give yourselves a half-hour in your rooms to freshen up, and then we'll grab a bite to eat," Egan ordered.

He walked over to the front desk while the students and Audrey waited in the lobby. A few minutes later, he strolled over with a handful of keycards.

He tossed one to Quest. "This is for you, Hugo, and Chuck. The room has two queen beds and a fold-out couch. You can flip for who gets the couch. Like me, you guys are on the third floor."

He handed Manya another keycard. "Second floor, as is Ms. Thorpe's room. It has the same set-up as the boys' digs." He pointed to Zina and Sienna. "Have fun, roomies."

Fawn and Charly turned to each other, horrified.

"Ladies, I can think of nothing that would make me happier than knowing you're burying the hatchet someplace other than each other's skulls. For the team's sake, I hope the next two nights will result in a peace pact."

He handed Charly the keycard. "Also on the second floor."

Fawn frowned. "Only *one card* per room?"

"No, there are two," Egan replied. "But your floor chaperone—that would be Audrey for the girls, me for the boys—will be holding the second ones."

Incensed, Fawn snatched the key from Charly and stalked off to the elevator, suitcase in hand.

Hugo grabbed his bag and went off after her.

Egan handed Audrey her key and then two others. "Your room is in the middle of theirs. That way, if for any reason you hear anything suspicious, you can enter at your own risk."

"Just like old times," Audrey muttered. "Considering how much of tonight may end up being 'don't ask, don't tell,' maybe it's a good thing I came instead of Daniel."

Egan kept his mouth shut.

He couldn't agree more.

Even if they hadn't been the only two people in the elevator, Fawn would have slammed Hugo against the wall and ground her mouth in his as a clue of what he could expect should he deliver on her next request: "Hey, so, have you got any Valium in your goody bag?"

Hugo snickered. "Of course, among other products: pot, coke, Adderall, some E—you name it. With all these competitors freaking out over this tournament, there should be a lot of takers."

He unzipped his bag, pulled out a baggie, and plucked two pills from it.

Hugo handed them to Fawn. Scrutinizing it, she asked, "How potent is this stuff?"

"Five milligrams. It's a knock-you-on-your-ass dose." He eyed her curiously. "So, you into that stuff?"

Fawn shook her head. "You know me. I'm all about all-natural highs and lows." With a come-hither wink, she stuck her thumb in her mouth.

He showed his anticipation with a giggle.

If there was one thing Fawn hated, it was a guy whose laugh was higher than hers. But if he were willing to give her the pills, she'd plug her ears and follow through with a little quid pro quo.

"Nah. It's for a friend," Fawn explained. "She's with one of the other competing schools. Why don't you leave a couple of them with me now, while we're, um...*alone?*" She twisted his nipple as an incentive.

That's all it took—along with a promise to meet him after lights out in the private room he'd booked the moment he found out the hotel Egan had reserved for them. "It's on the fourth floor," he told her.

"Sure," she promised.

But only as long as it took for her to slip him one of the

Valiums. She planned on crushing it into his drink so that he'd pass out.

Hugo Smallwood was a total dud in bed. He expected her to do all the work. And, ironically, living up to his last name, he gave her surprisingly little to work with. Not that it mattered. Better he was too zoned out to get it up than miss out on a good night's sleep before the tournament.

Yet another reason she missed Chuck terribly. When it came to sex, he always gave it his all.

Well, he wasn't coming back. She saw that now.

Her scheme to use Hugo Smallwood to make Chuck jealous backfired. Her ex was seemingly immune to her attempt to make him jealous. Instead, it now seemed he looked upon her with contempt.

Charly had won in splitting them up.

Payback would be sweet.

That's where the second Valium came in.

"Maybe Egan is right. Maybe we should at least try to get along—for the sake of the team." Fawn could tell her peace offering took Charly by surprise because the other girl quit brushing her hair mid-stroke.

The girls had staked out their sides of the room in silence. In a few minutes, they'd head downstairs with everyone else.

If Fawn was going to have her kumbaya with Charly, it was now or never.

"Being civil to each other would be better for morale, for sure." Charly's words were slow and wary. "Fawn, listen. I know we got off on the wrong foot this year for… for a lot of reasons."

"Only one reason, really," Fawn retorted. "Chuck."

Charly frowned. "Chuck and I love each other. And we respect each other. And, admittedly, I couldn't really see you two together...long term..." The second the words were out of her mouth, she regretted it.

From Fawn's wince, Charly realized the damage was already done.

"'Long term?' What do you mean by that?" But of course, Fawn knew.

"I didn't mean it the way it sounded."

Fawn shrugged. "Sure, you did. But, hey, if he was my brother and someone like me had him wrapped around her little finger, I'd feel exactly the same—insecure. Jealous." She put her hand on Charly's arm. "But now that I'm out of his life, maybe you can stop judging me. In a few months, we'll probably never see each other again."

"We may end up at the same college," Charly countered.

Fawn snickered. "Trust me—*we won't*. And in the long run, any memories we have about each other will seem like a bad dream." She shrugged. "So, at least for this weekend, let's put aside our differences. You know, take one for the team, as they say." She held out her hand.

She's right, Charly thought.

So, she shook it.

Throughout the team's dinner, Chuck did his best to keep focused on the group's strategy discussions as opposed to any chitchat.

Egan warned them that the participating teams wouldn't be given the debate questions beforehand. Once the questions were announced, the teams would have two hours to prepare their arguments.

He felt Egan had done the right thing by asking each teammate to assess the role they wanted at the tournament. Quest, Manya, Zina, and Hugo chose to focus on the research needed to make the arguments. Hugo's rationale was simple: "The last thing I need at this shindig is a high profile."

Fawn, Sienna, Chuck, and Charly were to rotate either the pro, con, or rebuttal arguments.

Occasionally, Chuck glanced over in Fawn's direction. It broke his heart to see her playing up to Hugo. He found it hard to believe that she was doing it to make him jealous.

I mean, come on already—the guy is the school's most infamous drug dealer! What's the future in that?

One thing that surprised Chuck: Charly and Fawn seemed to be getting along. Whenever Fawn interjected something into the group's conversation, Charly complimented her insights. Fawn reciprocated by deferring to some of Charly's suggestions. When both girls reached for the last garlic roll in the breadbasket, Charly insisted that Fawn eat it. Instead, Fawn split it and gave half to her roommate.

At that moment, Chuck felt there might be hope for their relationship—

Until she did something that curdled his stomach.

Halfway through the meal, he'd seen Fawn grab her purse and walk toward the restaurant's lavatory.

Chuck got up to follow her. He thought maybe they could have a word alone—

But then Fawn veered into the restaurant's bar. There, Fawn signaled the bartender for something. The man nodded, grabbed an empty glass, filled it with water, and handed it to her.

After she thanked him and he turned to serve another customer, she pulled something out of her pocketbook: a baggie. It contained some sort of powder, which she poured into the glass. She grabbed a swizzle stick, stirred the water, and then took the glass with her into the restaurant.

Chuck watched as Fawn moved the glass behind her so that it wouldn't be evident that she'd brought it with her. As the others laughed and talked, it was easy for her to place it on the table without being noticed.

With some sleight of hand, Fawn replaced Charly's water glass with the one from the bar while her head was turned.

Chuck was incensed.

What did she put in the water—a roofie?

Angered, Chuck was about to ask Fawn what the hell, but just then, Hugo leaned into Fawn for a kiss. Fawn glanced across the table at Chuck. Noting his scowl, she planted her lips on Hugo's mouth.

The kiss was long enough, and Chuck was angry enough to switch Fawn's water glass with the doctored one.

Chuck grimaced. Fawn was about to get a taste of her own medicine.

"Look, it's an Easter miracle! Fawn and Charly are getting along!" Egan murmured to Audrey. He nodded at the larger table behind her, where his students sat, eating and talking.

Her head whipped around. Seeing the proof, she let loose with a slow whistle. "Will miracles never cease—even on the Ides of March!"

Egan laughed. "By Jove, you're right! I've been so consumed with the tournament that I'd almost forgotten today's date." He tilted his wine glass at her. "Here's to a Shakespearean reference that few remember or care about."

Chuckling, Audrey moved her glass away. "I will not drink to that, and neither should you! The Sweet Swan of Avon is weeping in Heaven to hear one of his most ardent admirers turn on him that way!"

Egan laughed too—not at her statement but at the realization that Audrey was laughing and enjoying herself.

"Seriously, Egan, as inspiring a teacher as you are, you could be instructing at any university in the country." Her smile faded. "I wouldn't blame you if you left AA, what with the changes that are sure to happen now that Lavinia is gone."

"You sound as if you want to get rid of me." His tone was light enough, but he was dead serious about seeing how she responded.

"Not at all. I think of you as...a valued friend." She sounded as if she meant it.

"That means the world to me, Audrey. I would never do anything to lose your respect and trust."

She reached out and took his hand. "I realize that now. Thank you."

He was touched by the gesture.

He squeezed her hand tightly.

Yes, he thought, we can be friends.

But just beyond her head, something happening at the students' table caught his eye: Chuck was switching Fawn's glass with another.

He watched as the boy smirked at his former girlfriend and the new love of her life.

"Excuse me." Abruptly, Egan stood up. In a flash, he was next to the students' table.

Charly had seen it all.

The ease with which Audrey and Egan bantered and laughed together.

The look of longing in Egan's eyes.

Audrey's gentle deflection of his adoration with a mere touch of acknowledgment and a gaze of appreciation.

She knew now that no matter what had happened between them, her mother had decided it had no place in her future.

It must be devastating to love someone who can't love you back, Charly realized.

Shamed at her own voyeurism, she shifted her eyes away.

It couldn't have been long—just a few seconds. Still, suddenly, Egan was shouting at Chuck.

Fawn was picking up her glass.

Egan snatched it away from her.

"What the heck?" she exclaimed.

Everyone at the table turned and stared as Egan pointed to Chuck. "You—with me—*outside!*"

Chuck's face lost all its color. "But...you don't understand!"

"You're going to explain it to me—now!" Egan held out the glass. "Unless you'd like to take a big swig of this."

Chuck's eyes grew large. "No!"

Egan growled, "Why not?"

"Because…I don't know what's in it."

"If that's the case, why did you change out Fawn's glass so that she'd drink from it instead?" Egan asked.

"I'd like to explain—in private," Chuck insisted.

Egan's stare shifted to Fawn. "Okay. We'll talk in my room." He turned to Audrey. "You should join us." To the others, he added, "Everyone, back to your rooms immediately."

Stunned, the group made their exodus in silence.

Chuck saw me do it, Fawn thought. And yet, he won't snitch on me.

Knowing that shamed her.

She walked with the others back to their rooms, dazed by the knowledge that she'd just ruined Chuck's life.

CHAPTER 18

"What was in the water?" Egan leaned back on his bed as if to indicate they had all the time in the world to get the truth out of Chuck.

Audrey chose not to say a word. Instead, she took her place in the room's only chair.

That left Chuck standing.

And sweating. A sheen of dampness rose on his forehead.

He glanced at his mother. The look on her face—a mix of sadness and confusion—shamed him.

Finally, Chuck muttered, "I don't know what's in the glass." He raised his head to look Egan in the eye. "But whatever it was, I didn't put it there."

"I saw you myself, Chuck! You swapped her glass with the one you refused to drink from!" Furious, Egan rose from the bed. "Look, I know the break-up between you and Fawn hasn't been easy. And I see how she likes to tease you by flirting with Hugo. Still, I never expected you'd stoop so...*low*!" He shook his head.

"I'm telling you—I didn't do it!" Chuck retorted.

"But you knew something was in there. And you wanted her to drink it," Egan countered. "Am I right?"

Chuck couldn't deny that.

"If you didn't put it in there, then who did?" Egan asked.

Chuck stayed silent. But out of the corner of his eye, he watched as his mother bowed her head: in shame, he imagined.

"I'm sorry, but you're suspended from Debate Team," Egan murmured. "And when we get back to school, I'll take up the issue of your suspension with Miranda. If she agrees, it will affect your ability to graduate. I hope you realize that."

"Well, then it's a done deal."

Egan frowned. "What do you mean by that?"

Chuck shrugged. "I think you know what I mean."

The SAT test.

He's going to mention it here—now, in front of Audrey.

Egan's glance shifted to his son's mother. Her anguish had drained all the color from her face.

Instead of responding, Egan muttered, "You may go to your room now."

Stunned, Chuck left the room.

Egan turned toward Audrey. "I'm sorry."

"Do you think he did it?" Audrey voiced the question with no fear, no malice.

"No, I don't. But I thought he'd be honest and tell me who did." Egan sat back down on the bed. "You know I'll have to follow through on the disciplinary action. If Fawn had been harmed—"

"I know," Audrey whispered.

Wearily, Egan closed his eyes.

He could feel Audrey drop onto the bed beside him. When he opened his eyes, she was staring at him. The concern in her eyes touched him deeply.

"Raising kids is hard, isn't it?" she murmured.

Egan felt a lump rising in his throat. Still, he was able to mumble, "Yeah. Go figure."

When he bowed his head, Audrey patted his hand. "Thank you for believing Chuck. And thank you for loving him enough to do the right thing."

The team was supposed to spend at least the next hour on drills. Between the drive, the anxiety over the tournament, and Audrey's sudden appearance, the day had already been too long.

All Egan wanted to do was get some sleep.

And mourn his son's mercurial fall from grace.

He dropped his head onto Audrey's shoulder.

She didn't move. Instead, she took his hand and squeezed it.

They sat there, just like that, for a moment before she asked, "What did he mean by that?"

"Who?" Egan murmured.

"Chuck. He said... Let's see..." she thought for a moment: "It's a done deal."

***

"Tell the truth, Fawn. Chuck didn't try to hurt you. Am I right?" Charly flopped down on Fawn's bed so that the girl would have to look her in the eye.

Fawn had been crying since they walked into the room. Charly should have felt sympathy. What Chuck tried to do was horrendous.

But that's just it. Charly wasn't sympathetic.

She was suspicious.

Fawn's sobs died away. She did her best to wipe her face with the palm of her hand, only to smear the mascara already running down her cheeks in damp black trails. "No. He was just trying to save…" Ashamed, she dropped her head. "The glass was meant for you. I'd doctored it with a Valium. It would have knocked you out through the morning, and—"

Charly was too astonished to speak.

At first, she wanted to laugh.

Then she wanted to slug Fawn.

She settled for asking, "Bitch! Like… *What were you thinking?*"

"That, finally, you'd be out of the running, and I'd outshine you!" Fawn fell back onto her pillows. "Do you know what it's like living in the shadow of someone who's so—so perfect? It's always been like that with you! You're the perfect student. The perfect friend. The perfect daughter. You were even the perfect granddaughter—"

"Lavinia never played favorites!" Charly retorted.

"That's the point! She didn't have to!" Fawn shook her head in exasperation. Suddenly, she was crying again. "And you were—*are*—the perfect sister too."

She was crying so hard that she heaved.

Charly couldn't help it. She felt sorry for her. As she put her arms around the girl, she muttered, "Jesus, Fawn…"

The crying went on for so long that Charly was worried Fawn would never stop. When the sobs finally subsided, Charly whispered, "What do you want to do now?"

Fawn shrugged. "It's not exactly up to me, is it?"

"Yes, it is." Charly leaned back on the headboard. "You just bitched to me about how you see me as 'perfect.' Well, here's your chance to be 'Charly.'" She sighed. "So, what would Charly do?"

Fawn sighed. "She–*you*—would tell Egan the truth and let the chips fall where they may."

Charly nodded. "Well, there you go. So now, what will *you* do?"

Fawn opened her mouth to speak—

But there was a knock on the door.

Charly got up to open it.

Daniel stood out front. "High, gorgeous." He gave her a kiss on the forehead.

Surprised, Charly stepped out, pulling the door behind her. "Wow, you came after all!" She looked around, perplexed, "Where's Noah?"

Daniel grimaced. "He's at a sleepover. Something came up that… It needs your mother's attention." He looked at the door. "Is she in there with you?"

Charly shook her head. "No, just Fawn. We're, um… getting ready to meet the others for rehearsal."

Daniel grinned, surprised. "Well, that's…nice."

Charly ignored it. "Mom is next door." She nodded to the door farther down the hall.

Daniel shook his head. "I knocked there first."

"Oh… Well then, she must still be with Egan. They—"

"What's his room number?"

"Let's see. It's next to Chuck's, which is over mine. So right over Mom's."

"Sounds about right," Daniel muttered.

He was at the elevator in a flash.

The door was open—not entirely, just a crack.

Daniel nudged it open—not entirely at first, but enough to look in and see if anyone was there.

Yes, there they were. They sat side by side on the bed. Egan's head was bent over Audrey's. Their hands were clasped.

When he took a step closer, he noticed that their eyes were closed.

What. The. HELL?

Audrey murmured softly, "It's a done deal?"

What was a done deal? What were they planning?

Jesus—

Miranda was right.

It took all of three strides for him to reach the bed.

Egan opened his eyes at the wrong time—just as Daniel's right fist hit the left one.

Egan groaned as he fell back onto the bed.

Leaping up, Audrey screamed, "Daniel… *What are you doing?*"

As Daniel rubbed his fist, he muttered, "A better question is what are you doing—with him?"

"We were discussing our…son!" Audrey retorted angrily.

"Chuck? Why? What has he done now?"

Something is very wrong.

Charly had never seen her father so upset.

A thought struck her: *Does he know about Mother and Egan?*

Anxiously, she grabbed the keycard and exclaimed, "Fawn, look—I have to go up to Egan's."

Fawn stood up. "I'm going with you. I need to tell him the truth."

The elevator took a couple of minutes. By the time the girls got to Egan's, Daniel was already in the room—

And Egan was nursing a bruised face.

Audrey shook angrily.

Charly stared, horrified. Turning to her mother, she whispered, "Did you tell him?"

"I tried, but he didn't want to listen." She reached for Charly's hand. "I'm sorry you have to see your father this way."

My father…

Which one does she mean?

Charly was almost afraid to ask.

"Tell me what?" Daniel asked.

Oh…shit.

Before she could answer, Fawn exclaimed, "Mr. McKittridge, don't be angry at Egan! I was to blame."

Perplexed, Daniel declared, "What are you talking about?"

"The water glass—I did it, not Chuck. I was the one that put the Valium in there. It was meant for"—Fawn blushed—"for Charly. Chuck must have seen me do it, and he wanted to stop me."

"No, really, I wanted to teach you a lesson." Chuck's voice came from the front door. "It was stupid of me. I should have just dumped the water."

"You were protecting Charly," Fawn pointed out. "Egan shouldn't suspend you. He should suspend me."

"Don't tempt me." Egan warned her. He rose from the bed. "As much as you'd like to believe I was moved by your confession, I'm just being practical. Ashbury Academy deserves your best. *Lavinia deserves it*, God rest her soul. So, since no one got drugged, maimed, or killed, all your idiotic acts committed in the name of love, hate, or vengeance are absolved, and the confessional is now officially closed." Reaching for the ice bucket, Egan added, "Breakfast is at seven, at which time our tournament questions will have been emailed to me. If you are not in the hotel's restaurant by then, don't bother showing up to the tournament—*and you can find your own way home*." He started for the door. "Now, if you'll all excuse me, I've got to grab some ice for this shiner. Unless you know first aid, don't feel the need to stick around."

He stormed down the hall.

A moment later, ice could be heard clanking into the bucket.

Chuck and Fawn skedaddled.

Warily, Charly looked at Audrey and Daniel. "Mom… Do you need me?"

"Thank you, honey, but no. Your father and I need to talk." Audrey's icy stare was aimed at Daniel.

My father.

Daniel.

Together, Charly and her parents walked to the elevator.

To Charly, the one-floor ride seemed the longest in her life.

"Why are you here?" Audrey's question to Daniel was simple enough.

Because Miranda is tearing down the school, one illegal act at a time.

Because the FBI will soon be arresting parents for helping her.

Because I don't trust you.

Daniel knew the answer he gave would be complicated. He took a deep breath, and started from the beginning:

He told Audrey about his conversation with Tallulah on the flight home from New York;

And how he got the firm's private investigator to check into Miranda D'Arcy and discovered that her previous employer had bought out her contract and sent her packing.

He mentioned his calls: first to his old acquaintance who was Rob Edelson's partner, who told him that the FBI had come looking for Rob, and then to his new acquaintance, Vance Melamed, who headed the FBI office.

"Vance didn't deny that his office was looking into Miranda—which is just as good as a confirmation," Daniel explained.

And, finally, Daniel told Audrey about his confrontation with Miranda, and how she told him she'd shifted his endowment donation to Egan into her concierge program's account to make him complicit in her scheme.

"That way, I'd keep my mouth shut," he explained. "But I told her I wouldn't. And I'm not. In fact, I've set up an appointment with Melamed for first thing on Monday."

Audrey took all of this in silently. When he was through, she replied, "Miranda had Egan drill the students involved. He was also their test proctor. Do you think he may be involved too?"

Daniel shrugged. "She didn't say. But that doesn't mean he isn't."

"You should ask him," Audrey insisted.

Daniel smirked. "Do you think he'd tell me the truth?"

"Of course! Why would he lie?"

"Because he may be involved." Daniel let that sink in.

"That's ludicrous! Why would Egan risk everything for —*for her?*"

"You mean, as opposed to you?"

She stared at him as if he were a stranger. "What are you asking, Daniel?"

"Audrey, tell me the truth: do you love him?"

He asked.

And I will tell him the truth.

"Not now," she whispered. "But I did, once. A million years ago."

Numbed by Audrey's declaration, Daniel nodded slowly. "So, you and he…were lovers?"

Tell him.

"Just once," she confessed. "A long time ago."

Daniel dropped down onto the bed.

Audrey sat down beside him.

"How does it make you feel, seeing him now?"

She shrugged. "It was odd at first—like a ghost from your past who appears out of nowhere. You recognize his features, but you don't remember from exactly where. Then, when it dawns on you, you see that it's trying to communicate, but you no longer talk the same language."

"You said, at first. But not now."

He was seeking clarification. She knew that.

He deserves it.

Fervently, she declared, "Egan and I are just friends. He knows I love you."

Daniel took her hand. He opened it to kiss her palm.

Then he held it to his cheek.

Audrey didn't want it to stop there.

For that matter, neither did he.

There was no need to rush it. Gentle touches. Languorous kisses. Meandering strokes. Each subsequent touch piqued their mutual craving all the more.

In time, their rhythm picked up. Damp with desire, she called out his name.

Ripe with lust, he entered her.

In time, frenzied gasps gave way to slow soft sighs.

As they lay in each other's arms, spent, she whispered, "It was always us."

If only she'd known this back then.

CHAPTER 19

Ashbury Academy's debate team had already eaten breakfast by the time Audrey and Daniel went down to the hotel's restaurant the next morning.

While they finished their breakfast, Chuck texted his mother that the debate team had received its tournament argument and was working in one of the hotel's conference rooms and that she was to meet them there.

"Do you want to join me?" She asked Daniel.

He grimaced. "Yes. I need to apologize to Egan—if he'll let me."

"I can't imagine he'd hold it against you. Like us, he knows it was a misunderstanding." She laid down her napkin. "I'll walk in and ask. If he agrees, I'll hang with the kids while you two talk in the hall."

He nodded. "Okay, let's do this thing."

Egan was surprised to see Audrey. He was sure she'd have

appeased Daniel and gone home with him. If not, she'd show up when needed, but stay out of his way in any case.

He didn't blame her. For the sake of her marriage and her family's wellbeing, she wanted to protect their secret.

Even at his expense.

So be it.

Despite Audrey's denial to divulge his real role in their lives, he vowed he'd always find a way to be there for them.

To that end, that morning at the crack of dawn, he'd sent a formal termination letter to his literary agency. He also signed the contract proffered a few days ago by the talent agency Davis had recommended, ICA. His agent there, Amy Sorenson, was already crowing that Davis had accepted her price of half a million for the option.

"We asked for an executive producer credit along with creator and screenwriter," she informed him. "The network is excited about it. By the way, can you send me your other books? There may be fertile soil there too."

He was fertile, alright. Mossy, in fact.

"Amy, send it now, and I'll sign it. And I'll give you my bank account number too."

Half a million was enough to secure what he had in mind for Chuck and Charly.

He made the necessary call immediately.

Audrey would find out soon enough.

He wished he could tell Audrey about it now, but he knew it wasn't the right time, despite the wistful smile with which she greeted him as she beckoned him to the door.

He excused himself from the students, who were already busy dividing up the tasks for the four questions.

"Do you need something?" Polite, but cautious.

Audrey's smile wavered. She'd gotten the message. "Daniel would like to offer you an apology."

Egan shrugged. "Would he care to come in and do it? I can't leave the students alone."

"He'd like to talk to you outside. I can watch over them."

"They aren't toddlers. They're here to win their debates, and they need me to help them make some important strategy decisions."

"Yes, I know," she replied coolly. "As you remember, twenty-two years ago I was in their shoes. I won my debates. Perhaps I have something to offer."

Touché.

"If he's willing to apologize, I'm willing to accept his olive branch." Egan forced himself to grin as he walked out the door.

"I'm sorry I punched you." Daniel held out his hand to Egan.

Egan nodded grudgingly as he shook it. "I accept your apology."

Done. Now let's get on with our lives: yours, with the woman I love and the children I should have raised.

As Egan turned to head back inside, Daniel added, "Isn't there anything you'd like to ask me?"

Egan turned around. "Like what?"

"Aren't you even curious as to why I came down here?"

Egan shook his head. "I assume... I guess I thought you were here to watch the twins at the tournament."

"I wish that were the case." Daniel grimaced. "Miranda told me about your affair with Audrey."

"My...*what?*"

Daniel stared silently.

"Daniel, I swear—I am not having an affair with Audrey."

"I know," Daniel admitted. "Not because I believed Miranda. She's a conniver. I figured that out fast." His dismay showed itself with a tremor. "I hate to admit it: I jumped the first flight I could to come here because of what Audrey wouldn't tell me—until last night."

Audrey told him.

Last night.

He accepts the truth...?

"She told me that you and she...I know you were once lovers."

No. She hadn't told him about the twins, Egan realized.

The muscles in his face sagged under the weight of his disappointment.

"Two decades was a long time ago," Daniel continued. "The fact that you still care so much for her...I'm not surprised. Audrey is unforgettable. I'm glad you've accepted her friendship"—he put his hand on Egan's shoulder—"and mine too."

Egan nodded.

"One last thing, Egan. Regarding Miranda." Daniel looked him in the eye: "What do you know about her college cheating scheme?"

"Her...*what?*"

"I have it on good authority that she's being investigated for bribing influential college staffers, faking extracurriculars on admission applications, and fixing SAT tests."

He's testing me. He wants to see if I know he's involved.

Maybe I can make him sweat.

Egan smirked. "I wouldn't doubt it in the least. She'll do anything to prove she can live up to the reputation she's put out there."

Daniel frowned. "You've drilled the students in her concierge program and proctored their tests."

"Yep, I did."

"Has she given you any special instructions—you know, in that regard?"

"Are you asking me if she's bribed me to fix the tests—specifically, your son's?"

Daniel shrugged. "Yes, something like that."

"After last night, I know you'd like to believe the worst about me. But Daniel, I will tell you flat out." Egan looked him straight in the eye: "Chuck earned his grade fair and square."

Daniel nodded. In fact, he looked relieved. "Good to know."

Egan wanted to laugh. But if Daniel had paid Miranda to fix Chuck's test, sometime today he'd be screaming at her about being hoodwinked.

However, if Daniel wasn't bluffing and the Feds were onto her, Egan knew they'd be knocking on his door soon too.

And yet, Egan's respect for the man would be renewed.

But that still didn't stop Egan from wishing they could trade places.

CHAPTER 20

$\mathscr{I}$t was a true tribute to Ashbury Academy that its debate team placed sixth in the state competition, more so because—as Egan put it to Audrey—it was accomplished without anyone dying, ending up in the hospital, or going to jail.

The praise could be spread among everyone. The researchers (Quest and Hugo) kept their heads down and pulled together enough statistics, facts, and citations on each of the four topics. Convincing pros, cons, and rebuttals were drafted by Manya and Zina.

And although each portion of the arguments were delivered by Fawn, Sienna, Chuck, and Charly on a rotating basis, it was the twins who were the true stars, keeping their cool under pressure while delivering heartfelt oratories.

Although Audrey was disappointed that Daniel had to fly back immediately after the tournament for an emergency meeting on some major case, she noticed that Egan seemed relieved that her husband had made an early departure.

"I take it you worked through your misunderstanding?" she asked him during the team's celebratory dinner.

Egan shrugged. "He offered an apology. I accepted it. Case closed."

But she could tell he was worried about something. "Did he ask anything out of the ordinary?"

"You mean, about us?"

"Yes." Audrey admitted.

"He seemed to think he knew everything already—at least, as it pertains to us alone."

This was his way of saying: *He didn't mention the twins, nor did I.*

As her eyes misted over, she murmured, "Nothing stays a secret forever."

He frowned when she said that.

He wants us to come clean about the twins. I can't do that. Not yet.

Hopefully, never.

Miranda had decided that Sunday was the day she was to cut bait.

Just yesterday, she'd heard from two of the college coaches in her pocket that acceptances were due any day now. And besides, her conversation with Daniel made her uneasy. By revealing what she'd done to Chuck, she hoped she'd scared him into silence, but who knew for sure? Those by-the-book types were her worst nightmare.

Realizing that the Feds were surveilling her phone and home, and looking through her mail, in February she'd ordered a few burner phones on the school's account and had them delivered there, along with a couple of laptops and iPads, all of which she'd take with her to Ecuador. From what she could tell, it was the only place without a U.S. extradition treaty that wasn't located in a desert or frigid tundra, or run by some dictator.

Then, from one of the new burners, she ordered:

- New suitcases, which she also had delivered to the school.
- New clothes, knowing the Feds were watching her comings and goings for suspicious activities; and
- A private car to pick her up at the school promptly at five-thirty to take her to the private plane that would whisk her away to her new life as a well-heeled fugitive.

Unfortunately for her, Miranda had forgotten one thing: that the debate team was driving back to the school after the tournament, where their parents would be waiting to pick them up.

Gemma arrived first—around four-thirty—taking an empty parking space right in front of the large picture window in Miranda's office.

With no curtains, it was easy to see inside, so Miranda ducked down. Damn it, she thought. I can't afford to be seen here today!

She'd soon be on the Most Wanted List for having coerced seven of the debate team's families to join her scheme.

Including one she had set up unwittingly: Daniel McKittridge.

At that moment, Jess drove up too. He was there to pick up Hugo—yet another reason to hide. The last thing she needed was for him to look in the window and see her staring back at him. To bide his time while he waited for Hugo, he'd come in and suggest a quickie.

But one look around, and he'd realize what she was doing: going on the lam and leaving him and the others in the lurch.

She'd have to hide somewhere—and quick. If anyone saw her and then mentioned it to the Feds before the plane was wheels up, they'd be able to trace her whereabouts, or worse yet stop her from leaving the country.

Miranda knew the perfect place to hide: the clock tower. That way, she could watch as everyone drove off.

She crawled out of the office on her hands and knees. When she hit the lobby, she ran as fast as she could up the staircase.

———

The team pulled up in front of Ashbury Academy just after five o'clock.

Everyone was tired and ready to go home. Egan was too, but as the others took off, he went inside the school instead. If what Daniel said was true, it was only a matter of time before the police would come for Miranda.

He pulled out his resignation letter and walked over to Miranda's office, where he would lay it on her desk.

———

The door was closed. Oddly, though, it was unlocked, so he walked in.

Odder still, beside the couch were several suitcases.

Miranda is here at the school…

Jesus! I've got to leave before she comes back to her office.

Egan hurried to the desk. He was about to drop the envelope when he noticed that she'd left her purse and cell phone on the desk.

A passport lay on top of the purse.

He flipped it open.

The name on it read *PUCCI TEDESCHI*, but the photo was of Miranda.

She's fleeing, he realized.

He stuffed the resignation envelope in his pocket. He couldn't leave it now. Otherwise, she'd know he was there.

Just then, her cell phone lit up. Silently, a text message scrolled across the screen

---

Our apologies! Flight is delayed, as the equipment is still in transit from its last location. New departure time: eight o'clock P.M.

—Galaxy Marquee Airline

Egan hurried out the door.

Chuck was unpacking in his bedroom when a ping interrupted the music mix playing on his AirPods. Now that the Warriors had no shot in hell of making the NBA finals, the only alerts still active were for his college admissions.

He reached for his phone and saw

UC BERKELEY

Then another, and another, and another:

UCLA
UC SAN DIEGO
UC DAVIS

"Shit!" He cried. "*Shit! Shit!*" Even louder, he screamed, "Charly—*come here!*"

Charly was already in the hallway—screaming.

The rest of the family came out of their bedrooms.

"What the hell is going on?" Daniel exclaimed.

"Berkeley!" Charly and Chuck declared in unison. Then, to each other: "Have you read it yet?"

Both shook their heads, no.

Anxious, Audrey grabbed Daniel's wrist.

Charly did the same to Chuck. "Okay now, together on the count of three—Berkeley first, then UCLA."

Chuck nodded.

"*THREE!*" Noah shouted excitedly.

The twins clicked the links:

Jubilantly, Charly screamed, "Accepted! *Yes! Yes!*"

Chuck stood there, stunned. "Wait listed."

Charly's elation faded. "Oh…Well, look at UCLA."

Chuck grimaced but nodded. One eye closed as he hit the link:

He smiled. "Accepted."

"Hit the others," Charly insisted.

He nodded. Then, one by one: "Accepted…Accepted…Accepted…"

Audrey pulled them both close for a hug. "Congratulations, my scholars!"

Drawing Noah in with him, Daniel clasped his family in a bear hug. "Ditto. And, by the way, Chuck: if you want to hold out for the final word from Berkeley, you don't have to accept any of the others immediately."

"I know," Chuck replied. "But…maybe it's time we split up the circus."

Charly frowned. "What do you mean by that?"

He put his arms around his sister's neck. "I love you with all my heart. But you cast a big shadow. I think it's time I quit hiding behind it."

Charly gulped back her tears. "So…UCLA?"

Chuck held up a fist. "Go, Bruins!"

Charly had been so busy unpacking her suitcases that she hadn't even glanced at her desk.

But now, walking back into her room, the stark white envelope on the tidy surface of her desk stood out.

She walked over to see what it was.

Background Labs

It was from the DNA test center.

Had Noah left it there? Or perhaps Daniel?

The thought that it might have been the latter caused her to flinch.

With each step closer, Charly's heart picked up speed. Her hands trembled as she picked up the envelope. But she paused and took a breath before breaking the envelope's seal.

Charly and Chuck were Subject 1 and Subject 2, respectively.

Subject 3 was Noah.

The Paternity Subject was Egan.

If their Y DNA—paternal chromosomes— did not match Egan's, their CPI—Combined Paternity Index— would read zero.

Only Noah's showed zero.

Whereas the maternal half of Noah's DNA matched Chuck's and Charly's, his Paternity Index did not.

In fact, Chuck and Charly's analysis read:

Probability of Paternity: 99.9998%

Stunned, Charly fell to the floor.

"Charly! Come on down! To celebrate, we're ordering pizza," Noah shouted.

She had to tell Chuck.

But not here.

Somewhere he wouldn't blow up. Break apart.

Cry.

But first, she had to compose herself.

Charly went to the stairwell and called down: "Can I go pick it up?"

After a moment of silence, Audrey called back: "Yes— and thanks."

Charly went back to her room for what she knew Chuck would demand: the evidence for her accusation.

Then she knocked on Chuck's door.

When he opened it, she shushed him. "You have to come with me—*now*."

The look on her face spoke volumes: *Just do as I say.*

Nodding silently, he grabbed his coat and followed her downstairs.

CHAPTER 21

"How long have you suspected?" Chuck's question to Charly came after a few minutes of silence, followed by howling laughter in which he anticipated she'd join in when she felt the joke had gone on long enough.

Instead, she stared at the floor until he got the message that she wasn't kidding.

Charly was ready for his interrogation because she knew it would be the best way to counter his denial.

What worried her most was what form his anger would take.

They'd pulled the car over a few streets away from the house. Charly felt it was better than divulging the truth on some park bench. If things got ugly—if he shouted or cursed or cried—she didn't need any passersby to stare. Or worse, offer them sympathy.

Charly started at the beginning: how, as she cleaned out their mother's old room in Lavinia's house, she'd found

Audrey's copy of *Extracurricular* and read the inscription Egan had written inside.

Then she pulled out the book and showed it to him so that he could read it as well.

Chuck was silent as his eyes scanned the page. Finally, he muttered, "He was flirting with her. Big deal! Guys do that all the time. Hell, *I do it...*"

The similarity stopped him cold.

"All guys flirt," he insisted.

"Dad doesn't," Charly countered. "Not even when strange women come on to him."

"He flirts with Mom," Chuck argued.

"No. *He shows her he loves her.* He's not afraid to hold her hand or to hug her or kiss her in public. That is not flirting."

"You're making too big of a deal about this," he protested.

Then Charly showed him the photo contact sheet of Egan from the year he taught their mother. Seeing the red heart drawn around Egan's face, Chuck blanched.

He shook his head, dismayed. He shrugged. "Girlhood crush. No biggie."

Finally, she opened their DNA results from the envelope. "Remember when I asked for your spit? It really wasn't for a science class experiment. It was for a paternity test."

Chuck guffawed. "But—for that, you'd need DNA from Egan and Dad too! How—"

"Egan brushes his teeth after lunch. I swapped out his toothbrush. Most importantly, Noah's sample shows that we have different fathers." She pulled out the information sheet provided with the test results. "Read this."

Chuck stared down at it.

When, finally, he spoke, she could barely make out his words: "Does Egan know?"

"I have no idea," Charly admitted. "Why don't we go ask him?"

Egan flinched at the sound of the doorbell.

He fully anticipated he was to be arrested. And yet, he hadn't expected it to take place so soon.

Or that they'd be so polite about it.

Egan assumed it would happen just like in the movies —that someone would bark, "FBI! Open up!..." a second before the door was shattered with a battering ram.

He peeked out the keyhole. Chuck and Charly were standing there.

My God—has something happened to Audrey?

He flung open the door. "Is everything okay?"

The twins traded glances.

Chuck coughed uneasily, "Egan, um... mind, if we talk?"

"Of course not." Egan moved to one side.

They walked in, looking around cautiously.

Egan could tell they were uncomfortable. Finally, he ventured, "Has something bad happened?"

Charly exclaimed, "No!" at the same time Chuck replied, "Yes!" Then they traded responses. Perplexed, they stared at each other.

Until Charly blurted it out: "You're our father."

Oh, hell, Egan thought.

"Does your mother know?" Egan asked.

Chuck gawked. "What? *That you're our dad*? I would guess so! I mean…she's not stupid about *that* kind of stuff." A thought dawned on him. "Are you saying she was a slut?" At a loss for what to say next, he turned to Charly.

"No, of course not!" Egan exclaimed. "My God! She was—*is*—anything but that! What I mean to ask is, does your mom know that you're here?"

"No!" Charly replied. "We just now found out ourselves. And we thought that if you'd been kept in the dark too, you'd…well, that you'd want to know too."

As if proving the point, Charly turned off her cell phone, which had been buzzing persistently since they got there.

Audrey is trying to find them. But they're here. They're asking questions.

He'd dreamt of this moment. Damn it—why hadn't he prepared for it?

Here goes nothing.

"I knew," Egan admitted. "But only since before Thanksgiving."

Charly's jaw dropped open. "And…you didn't tell us?" she sputtered.

"Your mother asked me not to," Egan pointed out. "She felt it was something that should happen at a later date."

"When?" Chuck retorted. "When she was dead—*or you?*"

"That's a good question," Egan admitted. "Once I found out, I was shocked, certainly. But I was also willing and open to taking on the responsibility of—I wanted to be your father."

"Then you should have, despite what she wanted."

Charly's voice trembled with pain. "That's what Dad—I mean, Daniel would have done."

Egan looked sharply at her. "Would he? Do you really think that he would have gone against her wishes—which were based on knowing how much it would hurt the man who thinks you are his children? The man who raised you and loved you with all his heart? Whose every waking breath— *every action*—revolved around his wife and children?"

His words silenced them.

Charly whispered, "But doesn't it make you angry—that he took your place?"

"If you're asking me if she'd told me eighteen years ago that I was a father, would I have come running? Or if, instead, I'd have run away?" Egan shrugged. "Yeah, I'd like to think I would have manned up. I loved Audrey with all my heart. God help me, I still do! *I was just too full of myself to know how to show her.*" Suddenly, he was pacing the floor. "I thought that by writing it into a book and telling the world instead, she'd somehow get the point. But by the time we ran into each other again, she'd already fallen in love with Daniel." Egan winced. "But Audrey made the choice for me. He was the father she wanted for you."

"So, you met up with her again after they were dating?" Chuck pointed out.

"Yes," Egan admitted.

"God! That's so…*disgusting*," Chuck muttered.

Egan scowled. "I admit I'm not perfect!"

"I don't mean you," Chuck retorted. "I mean, our mom! *She wasn't loyal to our dad!*" He shook his head, dismayed. "The way he tells it, he loved her from the very moment he saw her; that he was head over heels in love with her."

Egan laughed wryly. "I know the feeling."

"And that, even when she quit seeing him, he knew he couldn't stop loving her; that he just needed to give her some space—"

"They had a breakup?" Egan interjected.

"Yes…for a few weeks, I guess. She was still at Berkeley, and he was already working for his firm here in the city. It was her senior year. Exams and all…" Chuck shrugged. "But then, one day, she showed up on his doorstep. He asked her to marry him, and she said yes."

Charly stared at him. "How do you know all of this?"

"Dad told me." Chuck shrugged. "It was after Fawn broke up with me the first time. He was trying to explain to me what true love means. That it's more than physical desire. It's when you realize that, no matter what, you never want to leave her side. *Ever.*" He glared at Egan. "Mom knew he'd be there for her, always. I guess she was right about you since it took you all this time to find out about us." Chuck tapped Charly's arm. "Let's get out of here."

Egan blocked the door. "Don't pass judgment on me. You don't know all I've done—"

"What you *haven't* done speaks volumes—or don't you get that?" Angrily, Chuck shoved Egan aside.

Egan shoved back.

The tussle ended when Chuck slugged Egan, and he crumpled onto the floor.

Charly knelt beside Egan. "Chuck—*this is our father!*"

"No, he isn't." He nudged her. "Let's get out of here.

"We can't leave him like this!" she insisted.

"Hell, I can!" The door slammed on his way out.

The last thing Chuck wanted to do was go home. Audrey was already worried. He knew because Charly's phone wasn't the only one she'd been calling for the past half hour.

And no way was he going to call back.

I have to tell Dad…

Daniel.

Chuck knew that if he were in Daniel's place, he'd want to know.

Once the shock had worn off, would Daniel still love them, or would he resent Audrey so much that it would turn his stomach to look at the twins?

For that alone, Chuck hated Audrey.

All his life, he'd put her on a pedestal. No more. Their mother had always insisted on honesty. But not telling the truth is just as bad as lying.

I need a drink, he thought.

Many of his friends lived there, in the Haight. He'd been at enough parties at their homes to know that the closest liquor store was a few blocks away. No need to drink and drive. Egan lived directly across from Buena Vista Park. He figured he could drink it there. Ruminate about the rest of his life.

The life that he now knew was a sham.

The only other customer in the liquor store was checking out the tequila shelf. When Chuck walked past him, the man—bulked up, frowning—was still glaring at him as he turned the corner.

The store clerk barely glanced at Chuck's fake ID. Chuck had just thrown a twenty on the counter when a voice behind him said, "I'll take that—and anything else you have in your wallet."

Chuck felt something hard against his side.

He didn't turn around. He didn't have to. The frightened look on the clerk's face told him what he needed to know: there was a gun in the man's hand.

Chuck put his wallet on the counter.

"Open it, you moron—and pull out the rest!" To make his point, the man jabbed Chuck even harder.

Chuck nodded. Still, with his eyes on the clerk, he slowly reached for the wallet.

The clerk reached for something too.

Whatever it was, Chuck didn't know because he'd already blacked out from the bullet.

An ice pack brought Egan back around. Through the one bloodshot eye that didn't hurt when he opened it, Charly's face came into view.

She looked relieved. "How are you feeling?"

"Shitty. Your brother packs a meaner punch than Daniel."

She laughed weakly. "Let me help you up."

With her help, he stumbled to his feet. They stood there, staring at each other.

She broke the silence by asking, "Can you take me home? Chuck took the car."

"Sure. Let me grab my keys."

But when they got outside, Charly frowned. She pointed at Audrey's SUV. "Our car is right there! He must still be around—"

Egan couldn't hear her because of the sirens screeching past them: two police cars and an ambulance.

Instinctively, their eyes followed the vehicles down the block, where it stopped in front of the liquor store.

Fear creased Charly's brow. The next thing Egan knew, she was running toward the ruckus.

Egan didn't think. He just ran after her.

CHAPTER 22

he call to Audrey came from Charly.

She could barely make out what her daughter was saying—something about Chuck and a robbery, and a bullet and all the blood—

And that Audrey needed to come to SF General as soon as possible.

To rouse herself from her stupor, Audrey washed her face in cold water. Then, as calmly as she could, she told Daniel and Noah to grab their coats and meet her at the front door; that she'd explain on the way to the hospital.

SallyAnne's mother believed the old wives' tale—that the way to a man's heart was through his stomach. Since her mother was an old wife and SallyAnne wasn't a wife at all, she felt she had nothing to lose to try it: specifically, on Lionel.

Melamed insisted that the cases would hold up better

229

in court if the charges went beyond intent. Until college acceptances went out and parents paid the requisite tuitions, arrests weren't going to be made. So, now, on a Sunday in which her case was in a holding pattern, Sally-Anne baked. Tomorrow morning, she'd take her culinary handiwork into the office break room.

This time, SallyAnne chose to make a dozen lemon meringue pie-lets. She knew it was one of Lionel's favorites. She could tell because he always took two back to his desk.

When her cell phone buzzed, it took her by surprise. She'd been placing one of the tiny pie crusts in its fluted ceramic dish.

She glanced over. It was from Melamed:

Maleficent on the run.

Oh…hell!
A second text read:

Pick up EG

Egan…?
Ah, the moment of truth has come.

He's at SF GENERAL

What the…
SallyAnne turned off the oven, then covered the rolled-out dough with wax paper and put it in the refrigerator.

Unfortunately, she'd have to dump the pie filling and meringue mixture down the sink.

She untied her apron before going for her coat, badge, and gun.

It was silly, she knew, but SallyAnne took three minutes to put on some make-up and a dress. Even if Lionel didn't notice, she knew Egan would, for what that was worth.

"How did this happen?" Daniel asked.

He'd never seen Charly so scared. She was shivering and hollow-eyed, but the streaks from the tears she'd shed before they came there were still damp on her face.

Daniel's eyes shifted to Egan. "And what are you doing here?"

Egan opened his mouth to say something, then closed it. Instead, he looked at Audrey.

Daniel, too, faced his wife. "Is there something I should know?"

Audrey shook her head, confused.

Charly stammered, "Mom, Chuck and I… *We know.*"

Audrey's lips went white as if she'd received a blow to the back of the head that sent her into shock.

"Tell him, Mom," Charly implored. "It's why Chuck is in there right now!"

"Tell me what?" Daniel demanded. "What the hell is going on?"

"Excuse me, are you Chuck's parents?"

Everyone turned to stare at the doctor standing behind Daniel. Instinctively, Audrey, Daniel, and Egan exclaimed, "Yes!"

Daniel glowered at Egan.

"The wound is not life-threatening. Fortunately, it hit muscle, so no bones or vital organs were damaged. But

Chuck has lost a good amount of blood. We need to raise his blood count," the doctor explained. "However, it will take us forty minutes to type his blood unless you're able to tell us now."

"He is …type O," Audrey replied. "Like me, if you need a donation."

"I'm O, too," Charly offered.

"Thanks, we'll let you know." The doctor took off.

Daniel stared at Audrey. "How could that be?"

Perplexed, she asked, "What do you mean? I'm his mother. Of course, I know his blood type!"

"No—I mean…my blood type is AB, so there's no way he's O… Or Charly…"

Daniel's stare pierced Audrey.

And yet, she couldn't look away.

Tell Daniel…about Egan.

"I…didn't know I was pregnant until after you'd proposed." She flinched, as if even whispering her long-held secret would send shockwaves through him.

She could see it had.

Daniel's head dropped to his chest.

When Audrey laid her hand on his arm, he shrugged it away.

Stricken with shame, Audrey shrank against the wall.

"Daniel," Egan muttered, "If it's any consolation—"

Daniel's punch told him it wasn't.

Egan slammed into the wall. As he staggered to his feet, he declared, "That's it! I'm getting a restraining order—"

"Mr. Gable?" The salutation came from a petite pretty brunette.

Pretty...

But vaguely familiar...

Perplexed, Egan replied, "Yes. Do I know you?"

When she held out her hand, it wasn't to shake his, but to show him her badge. "FBI. I'm Special Agent SallyAnne Jagger. We'd like to question you regarding an open case involving Miranda D'Arcy."

So, this is it.

In front of Charly.

In front of Audrey.

"Will you come with me, sir?" Agent Jagger nodded down the hall.

"I'm going with you," Daniel replied. The declaration slipped out before he could stop himself.

Egan stuttered, "*What? —You just slugged me!* You're full of yourself if you think I want you to represent me as my lawyer!"

Charly glowered at him. "Shut up, Egan! There's a reason my dad gets paid the big bucks."

As the color drained from Egan's face, it seemed to take his ego with him. "*Okay, okay!*" Wild-eyed, he turned to Daniel. "She's right. I... *I need your help, Daniel.*"

Daniel cocked his head. "No shit. But I'm not going for you. I'm going for my...*our kids.*"

"Jesus," SallyAnne murmured. "So...you know?"

Everyone stared back at her.

"Am I the only one in the world who didn't?" Daniel

exclaimed. He threw up his hands. "You're right, asshole. Call someone else."

Charly seized his arm. She didn't say a word, but he knew she was begging him.

"Listen, Daniel," Egan muttered, "I know we've had—have—our differences. But...*Damn it, I trust you!* So, please—will you represent me?"

Smirking, Daniel shook his head.

You're one audacious son of a bitch.

Then his gaze caught Audrey's. She too was silent. And she was smiling.

She already knows how I'll answer him.

He should have hated her for that, too. But he couldn't.

Once again, she's putting the children first, he thought. Just like when she chose me over Egan.

He turned to SallyAnne. "I'd suggest you read him his rights. Then we'll cooperate."

CHAPTER 23

By the way Daniel shook hands with Sally Anne's boss, Division Director Melamed, the two seemed like old friends.

Egan didn't know if that worked in his favor or not. For all he knew, Daniel might allow the Department of Justice to lock him up and throw away the key.

Melamed must have shared the same thought. His eyes grew wide when he saw Egan right behind Daniel. "Wait... you're now representing him?"

"Yep." Daniel shrugged. "Keeping it in the family."

Melamed's laughter filled the room.

Egan didn't like that.

By Daniel's grimace, he didn't either.

Egan's gaze went to Lionel before moving to Riley, then to Sally Anne.

I swear I know her….

At that second, it came to him. "You're the pixie!"

She stared back. "I'm...who?"

"At the bar, that night!" That awful, wonderful, life-changing night. "You were there when I ran into Miranda and she offered me the position of proctor. I now recognize"—he took a good look below her skirt—"your legs, even if you're no longer blond and in mourning."

SallyAnne blushed.

Egan nodded at Lionel. "Teutonic Twit was there too, at the restaurant." He turned to Riley. "And aren't you the mime from Argentina who was at Lavinia's memorial service?"

Riley winced. "I think I said Bolivia."

Melamed slapped his head.

Daniel took a closer look at him, then groaned at missing the connection. "Okay, now that we're all re-acquainted, I'm sure Mr. Gable has information that will help your case." He turned to Egan. "Despite any deal we cut here, a jury will have to convict you, and a judge will sentence you." Daniel leaned in. "Egan, the fact that you're sitting here is proof that they already have the goods on you, which, as Ms. Jagger pointed out, includes bribes for whatever tests you doctored for"—Daniel turned to SallyAnne—"how many students?"

She cleared her throat. "Seven."

"You're wrong," Egan declared.

Noting Melamed's frown, Daniel prodded, "How? Why?"

"I own up to changing some of the tests. Specifically, those turned in from Buck Crawford, Hugo Smallwood, Fawn McCoppin, Quest Wishart-Jammerhead"—he grimaced as he added—"and Zina Sisley-Calder." Egan took a deep breath: "However, I didn't change Manya Patel's score. She achieved it on her own. As did Chuck McKittridge." He turned to Daniel. "I mentioned that down in Los Angeles."

"Yes, we heard it," Lionel replied.

Daniel smirked. "I take it then, I've been under surveillance as well?"

Melamed grinned. "I'm sure you wouldn't have wanted it any other way,"

Daniel shrugged. "You've got me there."

Lionel continued, "And we also videotaped the testing session and what you did afterward, Mr. Gable."

"Good," Egan declared. "Then you'll see I'm telling the truth."

Melamed motioned to Riley. "Cue it up—specifically his actions toward Manya and Chuck's tests."

To the agents' mutual surprise, Egan was right. Other than checking Manya's test, Egan didn't touch it.

He didn't even look at Chuck's.

Lionel shook his head, awed. "Egan, why did you accept Miranda's offer?"

Egan sighed. "Literally an hour before, I'd just found out that"—he glanced at Daniel—"I was the twins' father. To put it lightly, it was a shock. At the same time, I realized how important it was to me to know there were those who, if by their genes only, were my legacy to the world." He looked down. "So, I resolved to do what I could to leave them some sort of legacy too—a financial one, since I'd blown any opportunity for it to be emotional. But I'd just been wiped out. Between my mother's eldercare and the Blackwell settlement—"

SallyAnne snorted. "Yeah, well, you have to hand it to Miranda. She timed that perfectly."

Egan stared at her. "What does Miranda have to do with that?"

Riley shook his head, awed. "Seriously, Dude—you

never figured out she's your old student, Mandy Blackwell?"

But then, seeing the shock on Egan's face, he choked back his chuckle.

———

For a moment there, Egan was sure he'd blacked out from his anger.

When he got ahold of his fury, it all made sense:

How, when she called on Lavinia's behalf, she'd mentioned being an alumnus;

And how she cooed about she and he "knowing each other in another life."

He remembered how she encouraged him to join the trustee board by claiming Lavinia would need his vote. She then had him nominate her for the board too.

All the while, she flirted with him, even as she was sleeping with Jess.

Even as she coerced parents into her program, behind Lavinia's back.

All the while she dangled carrots like the endowed chair while beating him with the cudgel of the defamation lawsuit.

She's played me every step of the way, he realized.

He nodded to Melamed: "Okay, let's make a deal."

Melamed grinned. "What do you have for us?"

Daniel nodded for Egan to continue.

Egan leaned back in his chair. "I'll bet you don't know where Miranda is now, this very minute."

"If you let us in on the secret, it'll certainly help your case."

"She's on the run—leaving now to catch a private plane out of the country."

"How do you know this?" Lionel asked.

"When I drove back with the debate team a few hours ago, she was at the school. I know this because I was going to turn in my resignation." Egan pulled the envelope from his back pocket so that they could see it. "I walked into her office. She wasn't there, but her luggage was, along with her phone and her passport. In fact, the airline—Galaxy Marquee—sent her a text about her flight being delayed until eight tonight. And by the way, the name on the passport was 'Pucci Tedeschi.'"

He spelled it out slowly as SallyAnne scribbled it down.

"You knew she was about to run. And yet, you stayed put," Melamed pointed out.

"You're right," Egan admitted. "Between what I'd done at Miranda's behest and what Daniel had asked me down in LA, it didn't take a genius to figure out you'd be knocking on my door next." He shrugged. "But I've been running all my life. The truth finally caught up to me. By that, I don't mean this, either. *I mean Chuck and Charly.* Had I run from the knowledge of them, I would have been the worst father ever."

Melamed nodded. "Thanks for the tip-off. Egan, is there anything else you'd like to tell us?"

"Yes. It's regarding the fees Miranda paid me for the students. Please note that the day I received the money, I donated it to the school's scholarship endowment fund."

Melamed grimaced. "Thirty-five thousand times seven...you mean, all two-hundred and forty-five thousand of it?"

Egan nodded. "Check with the receptionist, Clare. She

can confirm it. However, Miranda claimed that the money Daniel donated for my endowed chair was Chuck's fee. I don't know how that could be, since Lavinia was good to her word in making sure I received the lion's share of the gift."

"She discussed that with me as well," Daniel added. "I told her I was onto her scam and asked her to resign."

"We heard it too," Melamed admitted. "Now that she's Interim Head of School, she has pulled funds in that amount from one of the school's accounts. We're trying to trace its destination now."

"The judge may be lenient in Egan's sentencing since he didn't actually profit from Miranda's bribe," Daniel pointed out. "It's already happened in a similar case."

"You've got us there," Melamed grumbled. "Considering your attempts to redeem your illegal activity, we'll ask for a lighter sentence. But everything is at the judge's discretion." He turned to Egan. "Maybe you'll luck out and the judge will turn out to be a fan. Gentleman, you're both free to go."

Daniel received a text from Audrey: Chuck was out of surgery, and in stable condition.

"So, what happens next?" Egan asked Daniel.

"I'm going back to the hospital," Daniel replied. "I assume you'd like to check in with Chuck as well."

"Yes, of course! I mean…I was asking about you and Audrey and…the kids."

"That's between Audrey and me," Daniel replied stiffly. "As far as the kids go, in a few months, they'll be adults. I guess we'll find out how they feel about both of us, now that they know the truth."

The men drove back to the hospital in silence.

———

As promised, Miranda's private jet was wheels up immediately after eight.

And wheels down after only fifteen minutes in the air.

"Technical difficulty," the pilot explained. "We're returning back to the airport for maintenance."

She stalked up to the cockpit. After giving him and his copilot an earful about their lousy service and lousy planes, she stomped back into the cabin and fumed silently.

When they landed, the pilot suggested that she "feel free to stretch her legs, since the issue may take a while."

Miranda huffed as she made her way down the airstair—

Where a welcoming committee waited to greet her:

Lionel and Sally Anne.

Angrily, she exclaimed, "How did you know where I'd be?"

"Egan," Sally Anne responded. "Welcome back."

———

By the time Egan and Daniel made it back to the hospital, Chuck was awake: weak, but lucid enough to see them.

Audrey, Charly, and Noah were already at his bedside. When the two men walked in together, Chuck murmured, "I'd like to talk to Egan and Dad alone."

Audrey wasn't surprised by his request. Since he'd

regained consciousness, he'd made it a point to avoid looking at or talking to her, let alone answering her questions.

Silently, she left with Charly and Noah.

"I love you, Dad." Chuck's eyes met Daniel's straight on. "I'll never call you anything other than that. It's who you are and will always be to me: my father."

Daniel dropped into the chair beside Chuck. He reached out for the boy's open palm with one hand while he wiped away a tear with the other.

Egan tried not to stare at the tender scene before him, but he couldn't look away.

That could have been me, he thought sadly.

At some point, he realized Chuck had returned his gaze. Taken aback, he looked down at his feet.

"Egan, you will never take my father's place in my heart. But that doesn't mean my heart isn't big enough to open up to the place you hold in my life. To return your love. To appreciate your insights and your guidance. To know you have and will always have the best intentions for Charly and me." He attempted a weak smile. "I'm still a kid. I've fallen *in* love too many times. But when it comes to loving someone outright and with all my heart, there have only been four others: Mom, Dad, Charly, and Noah…" He stopped himself. "No, make that five. God, I loved Lavinia! I miss her now and every day. I hope I never feel differently!" Not willing to take his one good hand from Daniel's grasp, he shook his head so that his tears would break free from the lashes under his eyes. "If she were here now, she'd point out all the ways I'm your son. Don't think I haven't noticed it." He smiled. "I guess what I'm trying to say is that I want to love you too. And I know—no, *I hope*—that we'll have a great many years to prove it to each other many times over." He slid his hand out from under Daniel's and held it out to Egan.

Egan walked over to the bed and took it.

He kissed Chuck's forehead. "Thank you for that."

Then he walked out of the room.

———

"Eventually, Chuck will forgive you," Charly predicted.

Her suggestion, that Noah grab snacks for everyone from the cafeteria, gave her a few moments alone with her mother.

Audrey sighed. "I hope you're right."

"I know from experience. It's why I was so sullen these past few months—you know, after we cleaned out Lavinia's house."

Audrey frowned. "Why? What happened then?"

"I found your keepsake box at the top of your old bedroom closet. It had a small contact sheet of Egan. You'd drawn a heart around one of the photos—the same one that's in your senior yearbook."

"I did what?" Puzzled, Audrey tried to remember…

Mandy Blackwell.

Her guffaw startled Charly. "What's so funny?"

"I didn't draw the heart. Another girl did. She hated me. She even went so far as to steal a book from my desk that I'd used to research my debate topic. She'd used the photo strip as a bookmark." The memory brought a grimace to Audrey's lips. "It was Tallulah's idea that we raid her locker and take it back." She shrugged. "We also took her favorite boots."

Charly chuckled. "The Doc Martens in your closet?"

"Yes! *Oh, my God*! I'd forgotten I left them there!" Now Audrey was laughing too, which threw Charly into a giggling fit.

To keep from falling down, they held onto each other.

When their chortles subsided, Audrey gasped, "Goodness, I wonder what happened to *her?*"

"She must have been in your class, right?"

Audrey shook her head. "A class behind."

Charly smirked. "I wonder if she still goes by 'Mandy!' That's such a... I don't know, cutesy tweenish kind of name, don't you think? I mean—it's a nickname, right? For what?" She thought for a moment. "Amanda? Miranda?..."

Miranda.

MIRANDA D'ARCY.

The hair was different: blond and straight as opposed to red and curly.

She was no longer dumpy, but what had Bliss said? "Oh yeah: "She's had some work done on her face, and God knows where else..."

But the height was the same.

And that voice, too—when it wasn't drenched in syrupy sweetness.

And now this.

I need to tell Daniel as soon as possible.

She looked up to see Charly frowning at her. "Mom, what's going to happen to you and Dad?"

"He and I... Frankly, I don't know, honey. We need to talk." Audrey blinked away her tears. "He has every right to feel used. And I have no excuse for what I did, other than to say I didn't know I was pregnant until after I accepted his marriage proposal."

"Well, that counts for something."

Audrey pulled her daughter close for a hug. "We shall see."

245

*R*ealizing that their parents needed time to talk alone, Charly suggested that she take Noah out for pizza.

Noah knew this too. Before driving off, he took one of his parents' hands in each of his. Squeezing tightly, he said softly, "I love you—both."

Audrey and Daniel drove home in silence. She assumed he was waiting for her to say something, but she didn't know where to begin.

After opening the front door, he let her walk through first. He followed her into the living room, to their favorite spot: the couch facing the fireplace. It was the first piece of furniture they'd purchased as a couple. The cushions had been replaced twice, but the fabric, originally a colorful brocade, was now fading.

Every now and then Audrey thought of replacing it. But it felt as if she'd also be tossing away eighteen years of memories they'd shared, and conversations they'd had, as they sat there, side by side.

Tonight, though, they sat on opposite ends.

It's just like our marriage, Audrey thought sadly. Worn thin by all the things I've never said.

Well, now is the time.

She put it simply to him: "Ask me."

He thought for a beat, then nodded. "Tell me everything. From the beginning."

So she did.

About how they met. And how they ended it.

And all the missed opportunities in between.

It wasn't easy: admitting what it was like to hold onto an ideal about love. Not the real thing, but the fantasy:

Egan.

"If I'd only known then what I know now. That we'd never have been a good fit."

"Why do you say that?" Daniel asked.

"Because he was used to it from everyone: the adoration; the flirtations." She grimaced. "I vowed I wouldn't be just one more AA schoolgirl with a crush."

"And because you weren't, he wanted you even more badly," Daniel pointed out.

"It didn't seem so at the time," she countered. "He made that quite clear, up to the very last time we saw each other."

"In what way?"

"He told me AA had been just a job to him. A way to pay the bills while he wrote on the side." She shrugged. "It must have been true because the one opportunity he had to kiss me—right after I'd graduated—he didn't."

"Is that why you went to see him after the book was written?"

"Yes," Audrey admitted. Tears misted her eyes. "How I wish you'd gone with me that night!"

"Do you think that would have made a difference?"

She guffawed. "Of course! Don't you?"

Thoughtfully, Daniel shook his head. "I think it would have prolonged the inevitable. You said it yourself: he was 'an ideal.'"

"And you were my reality," she insisted.

"As much as you'd allow me to be." He shrugged. "I tried hard, Audrey. Really, I did! To respect you. To honor your boundaries." He stood up. "But let's face it: they were there because of Egan."

Audrey frowned. "What do you mean by that?"

"When we met, you were in your last year of college. You were still a virgin because no one lived up to your ideal of him." He smiled wryly. "And, apparently, no one lived up to his ideal of you, either. But at least it made him money, got him some success."

"After he and I…after we made love, I felt ashamed."

"Why?"

"Because I'd waited too long for him! I wasted too much time! I needed to let others in. I should have let *you* in. I almost lost you!" She sighed. "And now, I may lose you again."

"For now, anyway." He smiled wistfully. "I'm moving out, Aud. I need some space."

Now the tears were flowing harder. She shook her head. "No, don't! This is on me." She stood up. "Please stay with the kids. They need you, now more than ever. In his own way, isn't that what Chuck told you?"

"What do you mean?"

"That, no matter what role Egan eventually takes in Chuck's life, you are and will always be his father? And that he needs you, now more than ever?"

Daniel cocked his head, surprised. "How did you know?"

"How could it be any other way?" Audrey smiled through her tears. "Daniel, I rocked their world. You can steady it again—if you stay at the house."

"Okay—but only if you insist." He took her hand. "Will you stay at Lavinia's?"

Laughing, she shook her head. "No. Believe it or not, we've already received an offer! It came while Chuck was in surgery." She shrugged. "Full asking price, sight unseen. Cash deal, so no escrow. Of course, I told the realtor we accepted. She suggested that I hand the keys to the new owner in person, tomorrow. That way—let me put it the way she did: 'The person who knows it best can walk them through all of its idiosyncrasies.'"

"The joys of San Francisco real estate. Even a fixer-upper sells itself." Daniel shook his head in disbelief.

They kissed.

Audrey could tell that, like her, he'd wanted to linger in the memory of it.

She wished they had been sitting on the couch.

Audrey was waiting on the front porch of Lavinia's old house when Egan walked up.

Instinctively, she waved at him.

When he bounded up the steps, her puzzled stare was met with the grin that had once made her heart do cartwheels in her chest.

No more, but it still put a smile on her face.

"Out for a stroll?" she asked.

Egan looked down at his watch. "No. Quite frankly, I'm here to meet with…" He cocked a brow. "You."

She stammered, "But… Are you…"

"Yep." He leaped up the stairs and plopped down beside her. "So, do you want to give me the grand tour?"

After cleaning out the house, Audrey had done her best to stay away from it. The thought of losing it saddened her. Seeing it now, she realized the realtor had done a good job in staging it. It looked perfect: warm and homey, not at all ostentatious.

"I'm glad it's you who bought it, Egan," Audrey said. "You'll enjoy it here."

"Oh!… I won't live here—unless the trustees allow it."

"The trustees?" Audrey frowned. "But the school didn't get the house. It took the home's purchase money as a donation for Lavinia's scholarship fund."

"I didn't mean the school's trust. I meant the trust that purchased the house." He turned to face her. "I established it for Chuck and Charly."

Stunned, Audrey, murmured, "So, they now own Lavinia's house?"

"Yes." Egan smiled wistfully. "I've turned in my resignation to the school, Audrey. Davis sold *Extracurricular* to Netflix. The money was enough for me to buy the house for them."

"That is incredibly kind of you, Egan." Her voice trembled with her gratitude.

Tears welled in his eyes. "I can't think of a better way of

showing my love. And, frankly, it's too little, too late." Egan shrugged. "Chuck made it clear that I will never take Daniel's place. I don't think he realizes I never presumed I could. But he's come to the same conclusion I have about my role in their lives. If their hearts are open enough to include me, I will always be there for them in any capacity they'll accept." He took her hand. "How is Daniel taking the news?"

"He is…distant. In fact, Daniel and I have decided to separate." She stared out at the backyard. "For a while, anyway."

"What does that mean?"

"It means he needs space to understand why I kept the truth of our children's paternity a secret from him all these years." Audrey turned to Egan. "He has a right to take all the time he needs."

"What I meant by my question is, what does it mean for me? For us?" His eyes were filled with hope.

"Nothing, Egan. I'm sorry. I know it's not the answer you wanted." She held out her hand to him.

He took it. "You'll always be the one who got away."

SEVEN MONTHS LATER

Audrey had just drifted off, lulled by the Pacific Ocean waves lapping against La Selva Beach's sugary crescent of sand, when she felt a light pat on her backside.

She groaned, her way of expressing her displeasure.

She'd been enjoying her dream. In it, she was pregnant again: with the twins, she knew, because of the number of feisty kicks that thrummed in her full belly like a drum.

In the dream as in real life, the sensation had awed her, filling her with incredible bliss.

Audrey refused to acknowledge the culprit with anything more than one cocked eye. "Go away."

Tallulah waved back. "You know, with all that cycling you do, I could bounce a quarter off that ass and I wouldn't have to lower my hand to catch it."

Audrey laughed. "I guess I should I take that as a compliment."

Tallulah snickered. "At our age, hell yeah, I would!" She plopped down on the lounge chair beside her friend.

Gazing out toward the horizon, she declared, "God, I am *so glad* Maggie held onto this place—although she's come close to losing it on at least one occasion. Remember? The IRS almost snatched it for back taxes."

Audrey rolled over. "I'm glad she held onto it too."

"Me three," Gemma muttered as she tapped her iPad.

"Me four," Bliss shouted from the farthest lounge.

Bliss leaned over toward Gemma. "What are you reading?"

"Coverage on Seamus' trial. I still can't believe he pled not guilty! The jury is going to crucify that pompous ass."

Seamus' perp walk made the cover of the *San Francisco Chronicle*, and was picked up by newspapers all over the country. The laundry list of charges included mail fraud, wire fraud, federal programs bribery, and money laundering.

The charges for Jess Smallwood and Warner Crawford were almost identical.

Like Seamus, Jess had decided to take his chances and plead not guilty. Warner's guilty plea put him behind bars for eighteen months.

"If Seamus gets convicted, I hope he gets put away for a *looong* time," Tallulah muttered. "Between his plot to cut AA's scholarships to nothing, and to accept only parents who were willing to buy into Mandy's bribery scheme, can you imagine the devastation it would have caused the school?"

Months ago, when Audrey had revealed Miranda's former name to the others, the shock had been so great that no one spoke for what seemed like ages.

Tallulah had been the first to break their silence: with a litany of curses.

From that point on, they only referred to their nemesis as Mandy.

They wished they didn't have to think of her at all.

"Gretchen hasn't been the same since her prison stint," Bliss murmured.

"I would imagine not, after what happened to her there," Audrey shuttered. "Being tattooed by her cellmate! How awful!"

"At least they moved her into solitary after that," Gemma pointed out. "I'm just glad she was only sentenced for a month. With good behavior, she was out in three weeks."

Gretchen had been presiding over the Ashbury Academy fundraising committee when the Feds walked in the school auditorium, cuffing her in front of all her shocked acolytes.

In her case, the charges were negligible: merely mail fraud and bribery.

When Fawn's father and mother called her to bail them out, just out of spite she waited twenty-four hours.

"I'm glad Fawn forgave her after that," Audrey said.

Tallulah shrugged. "My guess is that there was nothing sentimental about it. Perhaps she thinks their mother-daughter dynamic will add more drama to her reality show."

It was no secret that on Fawn's eighteenth birthday, she'd been given control of a trust her father had set up in her name. The moment that happened, she thumbed her nose at all things Seamus and Gretchen and went her merry way.

CheerFullyYours was a goldmine. To make its success even greater, Fawn took a portion of her trust and plowed it into a large social media and publicity campaign for the website.

In no time, a television network had offered her a reality show based on her exploits. As fast as its audience was growing, the entertainment industry pundits predicted it would mushroom to Kardashian proportions in no time.

"I can't believe how quickly the Feds moved in on the parents," Bliss added. "Right after acceptances!"

"According to Daniel, the FBI felt it best to do so then as opposed to allowing the students to start the school year. That way, the slots could go to others who deserved them," Tallulah replied.

"I guess the upside is that it saved the students caught up in their parents' shenanigans from having to be expelled for no action on their part," Audrey pointed out.

"The one silver lining: since the FBI confirmed that Egan never touched Manya's test and her score was legitimate, Stanford honored its offer to her," Bliss reported.

"It was the right thing to do," Tallulah replied. "How is Manya doing, anyway?"

"The other AA students who also got accepted are looking after her," Bliss assured her. "And if Sienna gets accepted for next year, they'll room together. Considering how much money Raffaele donated to the school, her chances are pretty good." She shook her head, dismayed. "Donations are legal bribery, but still acceptable—for now, anyway."

Gemma frowned. "Too bad Nira wasn't told that in time. It might have saved her from taking her own life. What was she doing with a gun, anyway?"

"Her ex had threatened her on numerous occasions," Audrey replied. "The thought of losing custody of Manya to that creep was just too much for her." Saddened, she shook her head. "The money she paid to Mandy was the smallest of all the fees—only ten thousand dollars! I don't think the judge would have sentenced her to more than a few weeks."

"Any conviction would have been reason enough for the state to revoke her medical license and to get her fired from her medical practice," Gemma pointed out.

Audrey patted Tallulah's hand. "I'm glad Jammerhead took Daniel's advice: pleaded guilty and showed remorse."

"Me too," Tallulah admitted. "Rumor has it the reason he was sentenced to only a month behind bars is because the judge is a closet 'Jammerhead Bobber.'" Tallulah rolled her eyes at the nickname for her partner's fans. "His trial wasn't the best publicity, but it certainly popped his album sales." She grimaced. "So has a video someone made while Jammerhead was being arrested. It's all over the internet."

"It happened at the recording session for his next album, didn't it?" Bliss asked.

Tallulah nodded. "We always hire a videographer— you know, so that we can use clips for promotional purposes and for posterity. But this clip wasn't from that camera. It was a bootleg from the security camera."

Audrey chuckled. "For once, Maggie was right. Didn't she predict he'd come out of it unscathed? I think her exact words were, 'Hell, look at the cred Johnny Cash got from his arrests, not to mention all those rappers.'"

"Her own stints behind bars—albeit overnighters for drunk-and-disorderly conduct—endeared her to ex-cons, so I guess she's right." Tallulah shrugged. "Jammerhead does seem humbled by the experience. And it gave him the time to write a couple of killer songs. In fact, he's now going to a therapist. He says he wants to work out some of his daddy issues before it ruins his relationship with Quest."

"How is Quest's tour going?" Bliss asked.

Tallulah smiled. "He loves playing back-up to Maggie. It makes sense, since he's been listening to her music since he was in the womb. He's even building a fan base. He did the right thing for himself." She turned to Gemma. "How is Zina?"

Gemma grimaced. "Still hating her father for taking away her chance to prove she could make it into a top-ranked university on her own. She refuses to visit his gravesite." She sighed. "Not that I blame her. But her boyfriend, Sven, has been true blue through this whole ordeal. He's convinced her to follow her dream. She agrees with him that she should take a year off to help me at my law center and then take the SAT again at a certified facility before applying next year. He also suggested that she embrace this whole horrid experience in her college admissions essays. After all, she was a victim of it —and the whole cockeyed admissions system, for that matter."

"At least one good thing came out of the whole experience," Gemma added. "Zina claims Egan instilled in her a fearlessness toward taking the damn test."

At the mention of his name, all eyes went to Audrey.

She blushed.

"How is Egan doing anyway?" Tallulah asked.

"Now that Chuck is at UCLA, he sees him often," Audrey replied. "He mentioned that Egan is adjusting to Los Angeles. Loving it, in fact. He's really taken to screenwriting. And having gone back to AA gave him ideas for a few more seasons of *Extracurricular*."

"I'll bet it has," Gemma muttered dryly.

Bliss guffawed. "Not a week goes by that *People* isn't running a photo of him and some starlet on his arm."

"He's the one person even prison couldn't humble," Tallulah declared.

Gemma snorted. "He wasn't there long enough! The judge sentenced him to 'time already served!' In his case, it was the one day he spent in jail before Daniel bailed him out. What were the judge's exact words?... Oh yes: 'I have not seen anyone who is less culpable.' It doesn't get much better than that."

"She felt that his having donated all his ill-gotten gains to the school offset the crime," Audrey pointed out.

"Bullshit," Tallulah replied. "I'll bet she sleeps with a copy of *Extracurricular* under her pillow."

"Charly mentioned that Egan is also going to therapy," Audrey offered. "In fact, Chuck offered to go with him."

Gemma winced. "Did Egan take him up on it?"

"Charly claims Egan is open to it. In the meantime, he's trying to understand why his obsession with me went on for so long."

"We are too," Tallulah teased.

"Frankly, that is the *perfect* place to start," Bliss exclaimed. "You know, in hindsight, finding out he was a father may have been the best thing that ever happened to Egan."

Audrey shrugged. "I'd like to think so."

It was her fault he hadn't learned sooner. Yet another reason to despise herself.

Gemma tapped Audrey on the arm. "Daniel says hi, by the way." She raised a brow.

Audrey blushed. "You ran into him?"

"Yes, in the courthouse. I'm glad you recommended that I let him represent me with the Feds. It gave me the distance I needed from all of Darius' tomfoolery. The only thing I can say about my dearly departed husband is that he was smart enough to pull Mandy's fee from one of the many bank accounts we didn't share, so they believed me when I said I knew nothing of their agreement. In fact, I've asked Daniel to help me untangle some of Darius' other messes."

"He's a great lawyer," Audrey replied.

"And according to Charly, a great father too," Gemma said. "He makes it a point to have dinner with her once a week, just the two of them."

Audrey nodded. "I take Noah on that night." Admittedly, spending quality time with the children separately had brought her closer to each of them.

Recently, even Chuck had responded to her conversational emails with more than a cursory one-sentence response.

And Charly had divulged that it was Chuck's idea that they offer her a temporary lease to Lavinia's house.

At first, Audrey had refused. She was afraid Daniel would think it was a condition Egan had stipulated in the twins' trust.

Only after Chuck called her and insisted had she given in. "Just pay the utilities, and it's a done deal," he told her.

"And the taxes. I insist."

"Sure, if it makes you happy."

Hesitantly, Audrey murmured, "Hearing your voice makes me happy."

"I miss yours too," Chuck admitted. "Especially since you're not using it to scold me about something."

"Was I really all that hard on you?"

"Yes, for good reason." He chuckled. "But at least now

we know why. I guess I'm the one apple that didn't fall far from the Gable tree."

She couldn't argue with that.

Now that the sun was almost below the horizon, a chill had set in. Audrey grabbed the blanket beneath her lounge chair and wrapped it around herself.

"Okay, ladies," Tallulah exclaimed. "On our last day on the beach, please join me in a toast to our new tradition! Here's to our annual gal pal beach getaway!"

Reluctantly, Audrey raised her glass with the others. She hated the thought of leaving her friends for an empty house.

As much as she loved Lavinia's house, it was no longer the place she called home.

Family was home.

Things will never be the same, she realized.

She had only herself to blame.

Operation Sis-Boom-Bah was deemed an important one to win by the Department of Justice; so much so that an additional prosecutor was assigned: Jeremy Blake, whose record of convictions was second to none.

Miranda recognized the name immediately.

Her old high school boyfriend's limp—her final and most lasting gift to him—confirmed her worst fears.

Miranda's groan was loud enough to worry her attorney, Gerald Breslin. He hissed, "What's wrong? Are you sick?"

"No," she muttered. "Just doomed."

Her prediction proved right.

Despite Breslin's argument that Miranda's cooperation

had led to the arrests and convictions of those willing to partake in one of the largest college bribery cases in the country's history, Jeremy's argument—now honed far beyond his debate team skillset—proved much more convincing.

Miranda winced as Jeremy's voice boomed through the courtroom:

"Miranda D'Arcy preyed on the fears of parents who entrusted her with the future and wellbeing of their children. She created the web of deceit, and then entangled them in it. None of this would have happened if it weren't for her."

He walked toward the judge. "These are not victimless crimes. These are crimes that will resonate for years to come in the lives of those whose futures have been impacted by Miranda D'Arcy's actions."

Jeremy pointed to Miranda: "Isn't it time to impact her future as well?"

The judge agreed.

Despite Miranda's cooperation with the FBI, the judge felt the charges—obstruction of justice, money laundering, racketeering, bribery, and tax evasion—and her attempt to flee the country were worth a seven-year prison sentence.

This time, Miranda had no one to blame but herself.

***

"Here's to a win for the good guys!" Lionel tapped his wine goblet to SallyAnne's.

"I'll drink to that!" She giggled. "Or maybe I shouldn't. I'm already on my third glass." She looked around the bar as if she'd be scolded for the indiscretion.

"You earned it; wouldn't you say?"

"I guess so." SallyAnne held her head high. "Okay—hell, yeah, I earned it!"

Lionel raised a brow. "I love it when you talk dirty to me."

"Then maybe I should do it more often, *damn it.*" Pretending shock, she put a hand over her mouth.

"I mean…in bed." There. He'd said it.

She shrugged. "That can be arranged."

For a moment, he quit breathing.

She stood up. Grabbing her purse, she added, "I'm through pussyfooting around. No more beating around the bush…" She stared at him. "Do those count as naughty?"

He laughed. "It's a marginal call, but sure. Works for me."

"Good, because I mean it. I want you, *Lionel Porter Polk the Seventh.*" She sighed mightily. "My God—that's a mouthful!" Suddenly, she was giggling again. "*That's what she said!*"

Lionel was laughing too. And following her out the door.

They'd both come to the conclusion that it had been worth the wait.

Despite the difference in Lionel and SallyAnne's heights, anatomically speaking all the various pieces seemed to fit perfectly.

And in spite of their differences in temperament—or perhaps because of it—their lovemaking ran the full gamut of expression and exertion.

Afterward, they both agreed it had exceeded expectations.

As the excitement of the day and the exhilaration of the evening gave way to exhaustion, they fell asleep in each other's arms.

SallyAnne woke to find Lionel watching her.

Embarrassed, she sat straight up. "I...I guess we shouldn't have—!"

"I'm sorry, but...*I didn't want it to ever stop*," Lionel muttered.

SallyAnne's heart dropped into the pit of her stomach. "You mean...working together?"

"No," he insisted. "This!" To make his point, he stroked her cheek.

Then he kissed her.

The kiss was so long—so deep—that she thought all time had stopped.

When their lips parted, she whispered, "Neither do I." She felt tears gathering in her eyes. "But...*we're partners*."

"Not if I take the promotion Melamed offered me."

SallyAnne sat straight up. "A promotion?...But...he offered one to me too!"

Lionel frowned. "When?"

SallyAnne's brow furrowed as she thought about it. "A few weeks ago." She shrugged. "I'd be partnered with someone else, so I turned him down. I couldn't stand the thought of not being with you."

Lionel took that in. Finally, he asked, "For almost four years, we've spent nearly every day together. Can I convince you to trade that for a lifetime of evenings and weekends instead?"

And that's how he asked her to marry him.

When it was Audrey's weekend with Noah, she made the trek on her bike north to the McKittridge home before they took off through the Presidio and over the Golden Gate Bridge.

With her young son as her guide, Audrey was learning the bike trails that crisscrossed Mount Tam.

Sometimes Charly joined their outings. On those days, Audrey blessed Daniel for instilling in them his love for this communal experience.

All these years I've missed out on this, she marveled.

But no more. Now that her secret was out in the open, she could embrace a different kind of life with her children. Never again would she dodge their questions or couch her answers in evasive terms.

At last, honesty was front and center.

As she rode her bike up to her old house, she was surprised to see another bike outside.

Not Noah's, but a woman's.

Audrey's first instinct was to turn around.

Daniel has found someone else, she thought. Someone who feels comfortable enough to leave her bike by our front steps.

His front steps.

Daniel had moved on with his life. There was nothing she could do but accept it.

I can't disappoint Noah, she thought.

She jumped off her bike and walked it into the driveway.

As she headed toward the steps, the front door opened. Daniel stood there. He waved.

She forced her lips into a grin. "I'm here for my date."

He grimaced. "Noah slept over at a buddy's house."

"Oh…" Audrey looked around. "Then I should take off." She turned to leave.

"Will I do?" Daniel asked.

"Do…what?" Audrey shook her head uncertainly.

"Do, as your date." He walked down the steps and sat on the bottom one.

"But…don't you have company?" She pointed to the bike.

"That's for you." Daniel hesitated, then added, "Noah told me about some of the trails you've been taking. The frame on your bike will be shot in no time, so I thought you might like this one better…" His voice died away.

But his gaze was as steady as ever.

"You thought right." Audrey eased down beside him. "I'm heading out in a new direction. Would you like to come along?"

THE END

More Josie Brown Novels

Secret Lives of Husbands and Wives

The Baby Planner

The Candidate

Hollywood Hunk (True Hollywood Lies series)

Hollywood Whore (True Hollywood Lies series)

HOW TO REACH JOSIE

To write Josie, go to:
mailfromjosie@gmail.com

To find out more about Josie, or to get on her eLetter list
for book launch announcements, go to her website:
www.JosieBrown.com

You can also find her at:

www.AuthorProvocateur.com

twitter.com/JosieBrownCA

facebook.com/josiebrownauthor

pinterest.com/josiebrownca

instagram.com/josiebrownnovels

9 781970 093056